BELOVED
FROM THE START

*The Death of Innocence & Restoring the Soul
from Childhood Sexual Abuse*

Christine Turner

All scripture quotations, unless otherwise indicated, are taken from the Holy Bible, New International Version®, NIV®. Copyright ©1973, 1978, 1984, 2011 by Biblica, Inc.™ Used by permission of Zondervan. All rights reserved worldwide. www.zondervan.com The "NIV" and "New International Version" are trademarks registered in the United States Patent and Trademark Office by Biblica, Inc.™

Printed in the United States of America.

Due to the changing nature of online dynamics, websites, links, social media forums and references, no guarantee is made of the permanent reliability of these references.

Printed in the United States of America.
Manufactured in the United States of America.

ISBN: 978-1-7335754-0-9

Dedication

To my sisters and brothers,
We all have the same story.
The beloved child was born. Evil came to destroy the beloved.
We are now free to choose our endings.
May the conspiracy of silence be broken, as you dance in His light.

There is a longing, a yearning within us, that hopes. We hope we can have what so many of those around us seem to have, an undamaged happy life. We hope, especially, that our children are safe from the fear and the evil of the situations we encountered. We wish every good thing possible for our children, for their success and happiness. We yearn for love, and dream of a future that is even bigger and better than where we are at this very moment.

My desire in telling my story, is that there will be understanding of a topic often kept in the darkness, and a connection with my story that will allow hope to arise in others - hope for healing, hope for healthy relationships, hope for freedom in sexual expression, and most of all, hope to love oneself completely and honestly.

I dream of rallying a movement of empathetic support and understanding of those who have not been abused, but want to be there for a friend or loved one. I dream about removing some of the stigma and shame, as I talk about, what was for 30 years, untellable.

I see invisible hands that cover the mouths of the children who, even as adults, remain silent after their abuse. The pain goes deep, and so the instinct is to remain mute, hide, try to forget, and above all pretend all is well. Yet the irony is that only by speaking, by telling and receiving the truth, does healing come. Using our voice eventually removes the cloak of shame that engulfs the victims of abuse.

I am nobody special, just one of millions whose innocence was stolen as a child. I do feel unique in that I have experienced a great deal of healing. During the last decade, I have gone through a process that has brought forth wholeness in every sense of the word - spiritual, emotional, and sexual. If you, or somebody you love, have been hurt as a child, having experienced sexual abuse, there is a commonality within our stories, and a shared history of struggling through pain. At the core of the struggle, is the belief within our hearts that we have no value. In our darkest moments, we believe we are worthless.

Imperative to the telling of my story is the sharing of my faith. It brought me healing, as well as the strength to share with others who have the same story. My hope is that like me, they too will find what they have been searching for. Those who are not sure about the claims of Jesus, please continue reading and give my story a chance.

I honestly wish I could leave out the Jesus part. It would be so much more palatable to the masses if I could share my story without Him, but for me to be healed of the belief that at my core I was defective, I needed to understand truths greater than myself; this is where my search for healing and truth began, and that is where He came in.

occur in your family or your community, or to someone you know, or to you.

Or, could it?

Is this event isolated, or truly an ongoing epidemic? Is the possibility of it happening real? Is it truly a problem? How big is this problem *really*, you may wonder.

Because of its very nature, it is difficult to pin point the precise percentages of children who experience childhood sexual abuse. Experts believe that sexual abuse in children is vastly underreported since victims are reluctant to, or unable to, talk about their experiences. Some fear repercussions, and avoid dealing with the feelings attached to the abuse. Many prefer to remain silent to avoid pain, and many are in denial, suppressing or repressing their memories.

Statistics done in Harvard studies indicate 12–35 % of women and 4–9% of men have had unwanted sexual experience prior to 18, and, even higher rates internationally.

Some studies indicate 1 in 5 girls and 1 in 20 boys have been victimized, with children ages 7–13 being the most vulnerable.

This explains a lot; why so many of us carry the unspoken 'it.'

I am a supporter of the "Me Too" movement, which is focused on sexual harassment in the workplace and sexual assault. I am glad victims are speaking out. The movement has kick-started a long overdue conversation. I believe there is an unintended consequence with this movement that has brought complacency and a trivialization of attitudes regarding sexual abuse. I see a trend toward classifying all sexual abuse under the same umbrella..."Me Too."

I believe many would agree that there are various degrees of damage to the heart and soul of a person, depending on the degree of violence and position of trust in the relationship between the abused and the abuser, and, this may impact the individual trauma.

2

There is a difference between inappropriate sexual talk, rape, being groped, or a priest molesting a child. All cause damage. All need healing. They all involve inappropriate, unwelcomed sexual advances; yet, each carries a different level of trauma.

The goal of my book is to use my story to illustrate the core destruction of the heart and mind and how it affects the lives of the abused. My desire is to show how opening the heart to receive God heals the wounded heart and restores the soul and restores us to our true selves.

CHAPTER 2

With Family, You Get What You Get

For you created my inmost being; you knit me together in my mother's womb.

—Psalm 139:13

BORN THE ONLY GIRL between two boys, I had a special position in the family. The only girl, and the only redhead, I was both the precious baby girl, and yet 'just a girl.'

I could get away with hitting my brothers and then smirking when they got into trouble for hitting me back. Yet, I had little significance in my dad's eyes, as sports was his god and I was only 'just a girl.' There was little hope for my Dad to relive his glory days as an athlete through me. My parents were young and poor when they had me in the early sixties. The year I was born, my father was finishing his masters degree in school counseling, and working part time to provide for his family. There was little money, even for food, and I am pretty sure I was an unexpected surprise.

Pictures show a little girl with a pixie cut of flaming orange hair, freckles sprinkled across her nose, dressed in brown overalls - the hand-me-downs of her older brother. Early movie recordings show me being gently moved aside, again and again, as I tried to get into the action of whatever sport was being filmed. My older brother was the star of the show as he hit the baseball off the tee or kicked the soccer ball down the field.

My father was a Job Corps career counselor in Utah, while my mother stayed home with the kids. The family lore is that both my parents knew within the first three months of marriage that they had made a mistake, but by then, my brother was on the way. Money was very tight, and my father also controlled the purse strings, giving my mother a household allowance which was a common practice at the time. Not only did he control the finances, but saying he was on the frugal side is very generous. The fights I remember them having were always about money.

My mom loved being with us. We would sing in the car on grocery shopping day, the one day a week she had the car. I remember the laughter when we received applause, as we pulled up to stoplights in our 10-year-old white Ford convertible with red leather interior.

There were high points.

"Daddy's home!" we would bellow as he burst through the door at the end of his workday.

I would rush to the door and he would swoop me up into his arms as I welcomed him home. I can still remember the feel of his stubble on my check as I greeted him each evening with what I called a 'movie star kiss.' My father was the guy who worked, often two jobs, and came home to his family at the end of his work day. There was little interaction with my dad as compared to my mom, though, since dads were pretty much hands off when it came to sharing the child rearing in those days.

The times we kids played with dad revolved around sports. We were welcome to sit with him and munch on popcorn as he watched T.V. Many times he would wrestle with us kids, giving us boxing or karate lessons. I remember giving my dad a bloody nose when I insisted I have my turn boxing with the gloves on. Five years old, apologizing in shock at the sight of the blood, I lectured him that he shouldn't have put his guard down. I fully appreciated the laughter of the rest of the family during this discourse. I was always observing the lessons to try to prove that I could do whatever my brothers could. The best fun of all was playing two-hand touch football out in the yard with the neighborhood kids. He would always assign me a sneak attack play since I was left uncovered; being estimated the weakest link as a girl. I loved the thrill of scoring an unexpected touchdown!

Those were happy times for the first eight or so years.

Fast forward to California, the Golden State - but not for us. My dad took a job, sight unseen, in a small town in the San Joaquin Valley - think dairy cows, immense fields of cotton, alfalfa, and corn, all baking in the 100 plus degree weather of the summer, not the palm trees, ocean breezes, and wine country, with perfect weather, as you might imagine California.

My mom, born and raised on Long Island, somehow thought of 'meadow' when my father told her of the pasture across the street from our house. When we arrived to meet up with my dad, after a two-day Greyhound bus ride from Utah to explore the new home he had purchased, we found ourselves in a subdivision of tiny, cookie-cutter, ranch style tract homes. Our street was across from a cow pasture with several black and white Holstein dairy cows contemplating us over the barbed wire fencing, To this day, the fragrance of cow manure immediately reminds me of my childhood. I still remember the depression my mom experienced as she struggled to adjust to our move. School was the big adjustment for me.

"Go to the back of the room, grab your knees and bend over," Mrs. Garmen said as she opened the accordion door, exposing me to the classroom next door to 'witness' her spanking. No longer was I teacher's pet, the "helper," placed strategically beside the boy who struggled in reading and cleaned his dirty fingernails with the sharp point of his scissors. Instead, I was at the back of the class, daydreaming. 'Swats' helped initiate me into the new school and the more difficult expectations of second grade.

California was full of hot pants and mini-dresses. My mom had gotten it all wrong with clothes that year. I was in plaid smocked dresses whose hems hit below my knees, which had been the norm in Utah.

I remember playing outside at a neighbor's house three doors away and looking down the street as his car pulled out. There it was, a little red 1969 Datsun, with a gold recliner strapped to the roof with bungee cords - Dad's chair; a ridiculous sight as I re-imagine it today, but one that made my heart clench in grief as I saw it pass me by.

When my father came back to visit, I threw a fit. My older brother had gotten to spend the weekend at my dad's new pad and I hadn't. Again, I wanted my turn. After much begging, it was decided my turn would be the following weekend. This would actually work out well for my mother because the doctor thought she had breast cancer and they were doing exploratory surgery to remove the lumps and to perform the biopsy. There would be one less kid to worry about as she recovered from the procedure.

CHAPTER 4

Death of Innocence

...and they have filled this place with the blood of the innocent...to burn their children as sacrifices - something I did not command or mention, nor did it enter my mind, says the Lord.

—Jeremiah 19:4-6

HIS NEW PLACE WAS dismal, but cool to me. It had a swimming pool! The new apartment that he had left our home for was a one-room studio with a small kitchen, a bathroom, a sofa, a dinette table and four chairs, and a half wall separating the bed from the rest of the room.

That night, I went to sleep on the sofa, covered by a twin sheet. My father had always slept with his bedroom freezing cold if possible, and that night was no exception. The window air-conditioning unit blew full blast into the room directly at me. Soon after I fell asleep, I awoke searching for warmth. As I thought hard to consider a solution, I knew there was no linen closet with extra blankets, no robe or beach towels to cover myself, so like a mouse,

I crept into my dad's bed, where I fell asleep in the warmth of his bed covers. As the morning light filtered in, I woke to coziness and comfort. My dad was snuggling me. I remember feeling a moment or two of happiness- joy even, because my dad was showing me affection. I was 10 years old and he had not been physically affectionate since I was little. My happiness soon turned to uncertainty.

Was what he was doing okay? He kept saying a lot of words, his tone was persuasive, full of words about showing love and teaching love, but what he was doing seemed wrong. He was touching me in strange and unfamiliar ways. It was like a dawning, a slow radiating change, as thought followed thought; awareness, and trying to make sense of what was happening. Instead of a dawning of light, it was an ever deepening darkening. I went outside of myself. It was like I was floating above the bed looking down at what was happening, as I prayed to God that I would die.

My next memory was extreme burning. I was using the bathroom and had never felt such an excruciating pain and never in my lower region; it was burning and unfamiliar and frightening. I finished using the bathroom and looked in the medicine cabinet mirror. My face had tears streaming down my checks and I looked ugly. There was a change in me. I was dirty and disgusting. It was a pivotal reckoning. Looking back, I don't know how I knew at the time, but I knew even then that I would never be the same. My innocence had, all at once, been completely and totally destroyed; my innocence had been stolen, and, my soul had been shattered. I went from being cold on the couch to experiencing an inner cold I could not warm away.

CHAPTER 5

From Innocent to Guilty

I am set apart with the dead, like the slain who lie in the grave, whom you remember no more, who are cut off from your care.

—Psalm 88:5

PROFOUND DAMAGE HAPPENED WHEN I was molested, yet because the wounds were not apparent to the naked eye, the damage remained hidden. If someone stabbed a child, there would be outrage, ambulances blaring sirens, workers rushing to render aid, and prison time for the perpetrator. Why is it that the majority of the time, sexual predators and the damage they cause remain hidden?

Abusers use anything - violence, coercion, and manipulation, to bring forth silence. The biggest lie abusers inflict is making the little one feel guilty or complicit. As a participant, no matter if it were by coercion, manipulation or force, the false belief is formed that, somehow, some way, the victim is guilty and to blame, or share the blame, for the abuse. A child's belief system is very concrete

CHAPTER 6

Making Sense of the Horror

hor·ror/ˈhôrər/noun

1. an intense feeling of fear, shock, or disgust.

INFORMAL

2. a bad or mischievous person, especially a child.
                              —*as described by Wikipedia*

WE HAVE ALL HEARD of abuse victims who suppress or repress memories. Often times, repression is discussed with scorn and disbelief. We hear it all the time. "Why didn't the boy speak up when the priest abused him?" and "Really, they just now remembered - 20 years later?"

These are but a few examples of what we have all heard. But to explain the phenomena, think about the defense mechanism of denial. If there has ever been a sudden and unexpected death of a love one announced to you, most likely you have experienced denial in a milder form. There is an inner, "Nooo!" and disbelief, an unwillingness to accept the loss that sometimes takes weeks or longer to process, but in that moment, is immediately dismissed.

Suppression and repression are similar to denial, but the focus is internal rather than external. A sexual trauma or violent event has occurred which is so severe the child is unable to make sense of it or deal with it. Therefore the psyche works to protect the child from the mental anguish. Suppression is an active effort to keep something from arising into one's consciousness, to push thoughts or memories' of the event from coming to the forefront of the mind. Repression is not experiencing the thoughts or memories at the conscious level at all.

In order to assure the repression of my memories and to try to hide the trauma, my dad employed hypnosis. When I came out of the bathroom, I sat on the chrome dinette chair in the kitchen area of the apartment. My father stood before me and held a coin in front of my face. He made it sway back and forth, back and forth, back and forth, as he spoke to me, repeating the same words over and over and over in a singsong kind of voice. I don't remember the words, but I remember the coin; I don't remember every detail, but I remember the burning sensation, the feeling of emptiness, and floating away in my mind in all that was taking place.

Over the years, I do not know if my lack of recall of this event was due to being hypnotized or just my mind protecting me. I know that I told two people that my Dad cuddled me, but was either unable or unwilling to articulate more. If I'd been asked if I would like to forget what had just happened, my answer would have been, "Yes, PLEASE, make me forget!"

My father was into psychology and had read books on hypnosis and had practiced it with my siblings, with little effect. Years later, at the age of 38, when I would miraculously remember what had happened to me, my mother would confirm that I was not crazy and that he had often practiced hypnosis.

The day I first told her about my memories, she was shocked and skeptical, but two days later while sitting silently in church, she said it came back to her that I had come home that weekend and told her that I had an awful time at my dad's and that, "He had cuddled me and I hated it."

Did she investigate further? No. Do the families of victims often miss clues of abuse? All the time. There is something within us that either finds the idea unimaginable or uncomfortable. The bottom line, and one that I feel rage over, is that families don't *want* to know. Naively, the assumption is made, that it would never enter our minds to sexually abuse a child; therefore, our trusted family and friends also share these same misconceptions and instinctually deny all accusations. It is easy to overlook the 'monster in our midst' if we blindly believe that everyone shares the same values.

Why? We read the newspaper about the latest reported abuse and we think that it couldn't happen in our family. We wonder how the family where the abuse occurred could be so stupid. Why did no one notice?

It has been said that sexual abuse victims are often abused twice, when the event occurs and when they tell and are not believed or supported by their families. The extreme of this is when both parents are actively aware of the abuse yet encourage it, and/or participate in or facilitate it. My experience was typical of many, because abusers often strike during a time of family crisis or transition, when a child is not being supervised, is lonely, or isolated. I was alone most days due to mom going back to college, our family was going through a divorce, and my mom was distracted having just had exploratory surgery for breast cancer.

The ugly truth is families don't want to pay the cost of protecting and bringing retribution on behalf of the child. What are these costs? Jail time of a son, dad, uncle, or grandfather, loss of income, and divorce are just a few of the potential consequences. The cover up begins because defense mechanisms kick in. You, as a parent, failed to protect; that even despite your best intentions, "*You failed*," is hard to swallow. There will be no family reunions, Christmas or Thanksgiving family celebrations as a family.

One of the saddest costs that many choose is that given the choice between protecting her child and being alone, mom just can't give up having a man in her life, and choose to sweep over the truth of the abuse.

CHAPTER 7

Coping with the Aftermath

Dig deeply, oh my soul. Bury deeper still. Hide. Invisible,
alone, silent. God says He is my father, protector, help -
where is he now?

THERE WAS A KNOCK on the door that Sunday afternoon. After returning home from the apartment, my dad's girlfriend, (my mom's ex-best friend), wanted me to go shopping with her. "Just the two of us," she enticed me to agree.

Prior to this, I had been lectured that I was not welcomed to sit with the grownups when they were chatting, let alone spend time in their company. I was very interested in adult conversation and wanted to be in both worlds at times. I felt surprised, and, oddly flattered, that she was there to see *me*, to take *me* to town and out to eat. I left my mom, wrapped in her bandages from collarbone to rib cage from her breast biopsies, and off I went to Hanford with my new friend.

Looking back now, I realize that this was the beginning of my 'special status' in the family. From my research about childhood sexual abuse, it is a common theme. There is often a specialness bestowed on the victim, a 'payoff.' Later, this can yield feelings of collaboration and guilt when we face the full truth during healing and realize the truth of this special treatment.

The realization of 'special status' and associated guilt is a large factor in the victim's struggle with shame. Abusers groom their victims. They actually prepare them for abuse. They often violate sexual boundaries slowly through pornography, and test for compliance. They establish trust with both the victim and their families. They make the victim feel special, like the favorite or pet; sometimes gifts are given.

I was sought after for the first time in my life. My dad's girlfriend and I chatted like adults and she kept asking me questions about my weekend - for which I had no answers. I remember wondering what she was getting at with her constant barrage of questions. I believe now that my father had confessed to her what he had done and she was testing me to see what I remembered. I remembered nothing.

At other times after that I remember going to my dad's girlfriend's house, locking the bathroom door and taking tampons out of the box. I filled the sink up with water and dropped them in, one by one to watch them expand. Odd, I know. I don't know if I was trying to communicate in a non-verbal way that things were not right, or if I was acting out by trying to understand what was, before the abuse, an unknown part of the female anatomy – testing and exploring these instruments. It was a confusing time of life in almost all areas of my life.

So what does Post Traumatic Stress from sexual abuse to a child look like? It varies, but there are definite signs. The first immediate result of what happened for me was withdrawal and a shutting

clinic each day. I felt huge relief when she got the cootie treatment, too. If the bullies were targeting her, then they might ignore me, and if they went after both of us, at least I was not alone.

I suspect, as I look back, that she was a victim of childhood sexual abuse, as well. She had graphic knowledge about intercourse and said that she had been present when it was going on. She spent hours at her neighbor's home, a couple of single bachelors who lived near her, out in the country. I spent the night one evening with her and got permission to spend the day with her the following day. I don't know if parental consent was sought or not, but the next day an old man, a family "friend" who the girls called "uncle" took us into Fresno with him. I remember him taking us out to lunch and buying us each a gift at the mall. After the shopping trip, he took us to a park. We were on a secluded dirt path away from the crowds and my friend told me that we needed to go play on the playground a distance away. I wanted us all to go together, but she said no, that her little sister was going to remain in the car with the uncle. I remember being very uncomfortable and trying to talk her into going back and not leaving her sister alone with him. I felt guilty then, and feel badly now, for not protecting her little sister. I hope I didn't sell her out for a Big Mac and a Barbie doll.

While it sounds like I was a timid kind of kid, 'confident,' 'leader,' and 'extrovert' are words people use to describe me today. I have all these attributes, yet it is still with surprise that I can say these traits are true. I would love to know what my teachers saw in me as child before the abuse. I think I was a happy-go-lucky, sweet little kid. I think these traits are probably God-given and present, even then. A charade is what it felt like after the abuse.

The long-term, devastating effect is that the legitimate positives in my life, the truly good, as well as the controlling perfection I would strive to achieve, always felt like I was wearing a mask. No matter what I did, accomplished, or said, it would never be enough to erase the shame. In society, we use the term 'shame' when we actually mean guilt. It should be "You chose to do something morally wrong, *guilt on you*" – meaning you should feel remorse or repentance for violating your own or God's moral code. Shame is a strong word. It defines the feeling of believing that fundamentally, at your core, you have no value. In my case, despite what the world saw, in truth, I was not lovable.

On Wednesday nights, we spent the night with my dad. He had moved from the apartment in Fresno to a little house near the school. I hated that house, and I hated Wednesdays. You might be asking if the abuse continued. I know for sure of two other events, but don't know if there were more. I asked God when I began to process all of this, to let me remember the minimum I needed to so that I would become whole. For most victims, memories are torture. They pop up in our mind like a demented, twisted, movie we don't want to watch. There are times that I ask myself if my dad had a secret hypnosis word he would use to awaken me and to molest me. I believe it is likely the case.

CHAPTER 8

New Family

The 70s real Brady Bunch
5 kids, betrayed by infidelity
4 parents, divided by divorce
Rearrange, a new marriage
Shuffle into bunk beds, A New Home
Apply lots of effort and pretend
The 70s dream of a happy family –
My reality

SOON MY FATHER REMARRIED and his bride was my mother's former best friend, his 'footsie partner' from his bridge games. I was thrilled. My new stepmother was good to me - kind, loving, and supportive. I loved her and was excited to become a big sister to her children. I wanted to be a part of one big happy family. The *Brady Bunch* was the most popular show on television and it painted a rosy, idyllic picture of a large, happy, blended family. This was the goal of my father and his new wife. I fully embraced this fantasy.

I believe my father realized he needed to establish a relationship with us kids. When I am at my most cynical, I think my father wanted us to live with him so he wouldn't have to pay child support. When I am being more positive, I remember the better things about him. This is a huge portion of the dilemma we survivors must deal with. Everything is not just black and white. And, often, you love your abuser and, only see the positive things.

The good about my dad is that he was wonderful to talk to when he was in the counseling mode. He had a knack for knowing when things were not going well with us and would sit us down for a heart-to-heart talk. It was always such a relief when we were finished talking with him. When we were done, we felt heard, understood, and validated. It felt as if the weight of the world were lifted from our shoulders. To this day, my brothers and I agree that this was the best thing about our dad. He was the one who pried out of me the bullying situation I was facing and talked with the school. It resulted in a grade-level meeting that I was not present for, but the results were miraculous. The bullying stopped.

My mother and I were at war, going through the normal teenage girl-mama-drama. I made the choice to go and live with my dad and stepmother. They wanted me there and life was luxurious by comparison. Because there were two parents at home there was a stability and daily routine that I craved. Part of the 'special status' that I received was a loosening of the purse strings for me. Each time we would go shopping, I would get a new outfit, almost weekly. Instead of being the one in the wrong clothes, being picked on, I was working my way up to the 'in crowd.' I was making more friends and getting kind of cute as I matured. My confidence was growing. I was blossoming.

As I matured, I also became a friend and confidante of both my dad and stepmother. Since neither of them had many friends,

I would hang out with them. Everyone knew I was the favorite. I think I got away with it because I became the third adult in the home. I was the built-in babysitter for the three younger kids. I would make sure all the kids looked great each morning for school; hair combed, teeth brushed, and matching 'cool' clothes. I didn't want any bullying of my babies. I was both big sister and assistant mama. By the time I was a junior in high school, I was cooking dinner for the family most week nights and doing the weekly house cleaning for a ten-dollar a week allowance - good money back then. It was a lot of work, but I relished the power I had in the family.

Unfortunately, and to my shame, I decided I hated my mom and would have nothing to do with her during this time. I wish I were told it was okay to love and have a relationship with both my parents, but that was not the case. While my mom never bad-mouthed my dad, he was not so kind about her. I was not encouraged to visit my mom, though I could literally walk along the sidewalk around the block to her house. When I criticized my mom, I would be given validation for my backstabbing. Perhaps they were terrified that I would move back in with my mom and say something that might send my dad to jail.

CHAPTER 9

The Beginning of Faith

I will never leave you nor forsake you.

—Hebrews 13:5

AS A KID, I have always loved churches. I remember as a tiny girl, playing with a little kitchen set in the Sunday school room. Baptist, Episcopalian, Mormon, and Catholic - I visited them all with the families of my friends.

I came to know Jesus as a 10 year-old at a Pentecostal Church I attended with my babysitter's family. It was a busy, active place, with people praying out loud, altar calls and loud shouts from the pastor. Now, this church was interesting! I was a spectator there for many months and have no memory what the message was about that Wednesday evening. All I know is that for the first time in my life, I felt repentant and wanted to know God. I went forward and asked Jesus to come into my heart.

I continued going to this church during the years of bullying. There I found acceptance and love. Unfortunately, the teaching there was that one could lose his salvation. There was an altar call each Sunday, with an emphasis on repenting for 'back-sliding.' My Sunday school teacher spoke about Jesus coming back for a church 'without spot or wrinkle.' My question to her was, "What if you had juusstt sinned and you hadn't a chance to repent yet when Jesus comes back?" The answer was, "You would go to Hell!" Terrifying! From that moment on, through zeal and effort, I tried to be a 'good Christian.'

I must have been saved a thousand times in that church. Each Sunday I would kneel at the altar and just cry. I would sob and sob, gut-wrenching crying. I prayed for my family, terrified that they were all going to hell. I prayed for all of humanity. Many times it was just a wordless wailing. I look back and think it was a great outlet for the pain inside. Wailing each Sunday was such a release! What a heavy load, I had for a ten-year-old, worrying about and praying for the salvation of the world!

CHAPTER 10

The Two Faces of Chris

We all, like sheep, have gone astray; each of us has turned to our own way.

—Isaiah 53:6

THE MICROSCOPE OF A small town; I felt under it all the time. I worried about our name in the community because of the infidelity and the breakup of our family that was made so public. The opinion of my neighbors mattered. How we dressed, behaved, and were spoken about by others was a concern. I wanted to prove we were upstanding and good people. Because of this, I actually became popular during my high school years.

Chameleon-like, I learned to observe, read body language and secret looks, always adapting to each situation. What did I need to do to fit in and be liked? I became a cheerleader, lifeguard, and president of the Future Farmers of America Parliamentary Procedure Team, which was the closest thing we had to a debate team. We would travel to meets and debate politics related to agriculture. Don't laugh. FFA membership consisted of the cool kids in my town. I was even first runner-up in the California State FFA Sweetheart contest, a high school beauty contest, and voted Miss Personality. This was an achievement I was proud of, however, boys in my town did not seem very interested in me and I never had a real boyfriend.

In high school, I was the good girl - smart and popular. But alas, I longed for a boyfriend. I loved 'making out,' but was very scared of 'getting a reputation' and having the community gossip about me, as they did during my parent's breakup. I had real internal conflict - whenever I went out with a boy I liked, I worked hard to remain a 'virgin,' but had extreme difficulty saying 'no' to sexual pressures.

Like a bird flying south, I would have seasons where returning to my faith was my home. It was all or nothing though. I would maintain my ideal of Christian perfection, quickly saying I was sorry for the slightest sin, evaluating, scoring, keeping track...trying to be good. Failure to resist temptation - a make-out session, or a night of secret underage drinking, would send me back to my other self, the bad-girl.

College is where the conflict within me emerged. I had never been sought after in my town and now, at college, I was considered attractive. 'Hot' would be the word in today's vernacular, but it was 'fox' back then. There was nowhere in my psyche that I was prepared for the men I would encounter. Young men, bosses, grocery store clerks, dads and grandpas were always looking at me, undressing me with their eyes. I was shocked, but also flattered. After being bullied and told I was ugly again and again in elementary school, I was thrilled by the attention and began to embrace my sexuality and my power. I discovered that female beauty is powerful, but also dangerous. At times, I dressed provocatively and had a sexual aura of femininity, and loved attracting male attention. I kept my good-girl image most of the time, except occasionally, when I drank. When I drank, my inhibitions were gone and I sometimes would give myself away and the bad girl would rule.

Two things were going on. One, if I really liked someone, I would desperately want him to be my boyfriend. Instead of dating for a period of time and getting to know one another slowly, I would give myself to him. I felt no purity or belief that my sexuality was sacred or precious. It was for the use of others, to make others happy. After he got what he wanted, I wouldn't see him again. He would spread rumors about me, bringing me the very reputation I was so afraid of, as well as all the shame that accompanies it.

Fill the room with men and my radar was like that of a heat-seeking missile, locking on the very worst of the bunch. I was a magnet for jerks - the bad boys. They were exciting, and after one thing. They treated me the very way my heart felt I deserved; like I had no value. I thought that nice men, kind men, men who respected women, seemed kind of boring.

Each time, I would be crushed. I had given him what he wanted, my most precious things, my kisses, my intimacy, the center of my body. 'Love me.' 'Choose me.' Yet, I was nothing to him.

War raged within me. My behavior was in accordance with my inner beliefs; I behaved in a shameful way, as though I were worthless. I would tell others and myself that I was embracing the sexual revolution. Women should be able to have sex for just the pure physicality of it, just like men. But that couldn't explain the conflict, turmoil, and disgust I felt the morning after. I could not enjoy this so called 'freedom' because it was incongruent with whom God said I was. I had Him fighting for me. I couldn't just 'have sex' and be okay. I felt remorse, repentance, and guilt, because I knew this was not the behavior needed to bring me a good and happy life. I don't think this is just a phenomena because of Christian and/or moral teaching. Intrinsically, we are created as beings of value, to love and be loved, to be and treat one another as treasures. Women especially, open their hearts and souls during sexual intimacy. Sexual intimacy is a sacred act and both the saved and unsaved feel the shame I speak of when we give ourselves away so recklessly.

CHAPTER 11

My Abusive Love

You get what you think you deserve.
            —My wise mom's saying

AS COLLEGE WAS ENDING and I began my teaching career, I finally got my wish - a serious boyfriend, and British, no less - someone who said he loved me! Red flags should have been flying, because he had the classic signs of an abusive man. He had seen me in our apartment complex and began leaving notes on my windshield saying they were from 'a secret admirer.' Notes and flowers appeared daily for a few weeks. Instead of 'stalker' and 'run for your life,' I was flattered by the attention.

We soon met, began dating, and rushed to move in together. Like most abusers, he isolated me from my friends and tried to alienate me from my family. My biggest mistake was telling him about my past. He used this information to batter me over and over again with his words.

The verbal abuse went on for three years. It seemed to happen most when we were driving in a car. Trapped, with the windows rolled up, speeding down the road, he would yell, cry even, and call me a slut. I took it. I tried to explain, appease him, and say I was sorry. Even with this going on, I was hoping he would ask me to marry him!

On Christmas, he gave me a ring, but not an engagement ring. Trying to act excitedly and hide my embarrassment while in front of my family, I opened my gift, a plain gold wedding band.

It wasn't until his friend was visiting from England that things came to a head. A letter had arrived about the status of his marriage and that it was time to schedule another routine check with immigration control to assure it was bona-fide.

What? Marriage? Immigration? Over the next day he explained to me, "Oh, by the way, I paid this girl to marry me so I could stay in the country." "Did I forget to mention these last three years that I am actually married? You shouldn't be upset because it is on paper only."

That night, when I asked more questions, he told me to, "Shut my M—F—ing mouth, you M F—ing B—" in front of our houseguest, no less. I went to the bathroom and he followed me. Squeezing his hands around my neck, he choked me against the wall, towering over me, red-faced, screaming and spitting, all six foot seven inches of him hulking over me as he berated me.

Not being a total dummy, I nodded my head in terror agreeing with him. As he let me go, I told him I was so sorry. Tiptoeing to the bedroom, I telephoned my mother and whispered to her what had happened. The next morning my brother and his friends were outside the apartment with a U-Haul to move me home to Mama.

Back in Riverdale for the summer with no friends, I'd reached rock bottom. Could life get any worse?

CHAPTER 12

My Prince,
Compliments of the US Navy

Every good and perfect gift comes from above and is from
the Father of Light.

—James 1:17

OUTSIDE OF THE FRESNO Air Terminal I ran into a neighbor.
She invited me to help her by volunteering as a camp counselor for
a Muscular Dystrophy camp. They were short counselors and as
an elementary teacher, I would be able to help them out. Having
nothing better to do, I agreed.

I knew little more about the disease than that Jerry Lewis had
telethons for Muscular Dystrophy. As I arrived, I was given my
assignment, three little boys who were about nine years old and
still able to walk. Older victims were wheelchair bound with a
life expectancy of around 25 years at the time. The disease attacks
periphery muscles as the body gives way, trying to protect the vital
organs, above all else.

It was so sad and I worked hard to behave normally. Soon, muscles built in my legs as I carried my fatigued charges piggyback around camp. Because I was a lifeguard and WSI certified, I was qualified to oversee the young men swimming, some of whom had not been able to enjoy the water in years. One following the other, we would lift a camper from his chair, lowering him in the cool water. Floating them around on their backs, cradling their heads and swirling them through the water, such joy and laughter! My heart was full.

Little did I know that during this week, I would have a pivotal God experience, though I was not aware of it until after the fact. Late our final night, I put my little guys to bed and waited until they fell asleep. Just steps from our doorway, was the dock on a small lake. I sat upon it, feet dangling as moonlight glimmered on the water. Not far away, moonlight shone on a nearby pavilion, music drifting towards me, as the rock-tunes provided the backdrop for the wheelchair dancers still in full swing. My heart was so full. Melancholy and joy were within me; it was bittersweet. While I longed to be able to change the destiny of the dancers, some who would not make it to next year's camp, I was grateful to have shared this time with them.

For the first time in years, I prayed. I prayed for the young men dancing in the distance and my little campers asleep in their bunks. And, as I continued, I began to pray for myself. I poured out my disillusionment and disappointment over my life. I was just so tired; tired of searching for love in the arms of jerks. I told God I was sorry for the paths my life had taken, that I wanted it no more. I just remember a silent sobbing as I looked over the water at the beauty of the night and broke. I asked for a husband, a good man, unlike any of the men of my past. I felt infinity as

I watched the stars, the light and the sounds of the night. Peace flooded me. Three days later I met my prince, at a bar.

Yes, I met my prince at a bar. My mom asked a single co-worker to have pity on me and take me to the local hang out, since I had no connections or friends in the area. I met her at the Cotton Mill, the local watering hole, the first bar I ever entered, and had to wait for someone as a lone woman, feeling very uncomfortable and conspicuous. A young, balding Navy officer with vibrate blue eyes approached. He was inviting everyone to his party the following night, a luau. We chatted, had two dances, and he was off to invite the rest of the patrons in the bar.

It was Christmas in July, and the outdoor Christmas lights flashed marking the location. There was a party at the 'Dog House', Jeff's home he shared with two other officers. I was eager to go, but not sure what to expect once I got there. There were people everywhere. Music bounced off the walls. Loud laughter and shouting surrounded us. Someone telephoned a bar in Honolulu to get the official Mai Tai recipe, while shrieks pierced the air as girls and guys were tossed in the swimming pool. Never leaving my side after being greeted, Jeff gave me a tour of the house. No bedroom tour? No 'come and see my etchings,' as I had heard times before. Instead, at midnight, he kissed me on the cheek as he saw me to my car. Such manners, respect, decorum; I pretended this was the norm for me. It was decided we would drive to Yosemite the next day for our first date, finishing with dinner in a nice restaurant. That date lasted 17 hours.

Three weeks together, and then six months apart, that was our test. Jeff was deployed on a six-month cruise and I decided I would wait for him to come back.

During this first deployment, *Top Gun* was released. I knew Jeff flew planes and landed on aircraft carriers, but I was impressed even more when I saw the movie. My boyfriend was my very own Tom Cruise, but taller!

As we dated, I kept being surprised. He could fix anything and he didn't cuss and scream if a project didn't go right. While straight-laced and moral, he did not believe in God. He was funny and would make friends wherever we went. His kindness and generosity weren't just for me, but for everyone; it was genuinely who he was. Waitresses loved him and he was friendly with the garbage man, too.

Little things like holding the door for women and rushing to help if someone were struggling with their arms full were second nature to him. To this day he opens my door and refuses to sit at the table until all the women are seated.

We dated for another year and were married in the base chapel. My father sobbed through the entire ceremony. Later he told me he felt he was losing me, and that I had selected a man the complete opposite of him. By God's grace, in the ways that matter most, I had.

No one really knows exactly whom he or she is marrying. We only show our shiny best side. Men no longer like to dance - 'a mating ritual' my husband calls it. Women actually can eat the entire giant cheeseburger served in a restaurant. But I made sure Jeff did not fully know the 'real me.' The details of some of my past and my former living arrangement with my ex-boyfriend were my big secrets. I had learned my lesson. If you tell someone about your sins, they will use it against you to beat you down. I insinuated that I was a 'good girl' with not much sexual experience. Luckily, Jeff's belief was, 'the past doesn't matter'; neither of us were innocent and our histories with the opposite sex did not need hashing out.

After a second deployment and being together only three

months of our first year of marriage, we made the decision, that for our future family's sake, we would leave the Navy. It was Good Friday and I was nine-months pregnant; we screamed in disbelief when we got the call. Thrilled does not describe it when Jeff was hired by the airlines and Atlanta is where we landed.

A beautiful baby boy, followed two years later with a blue-eyed baby girl, a brown and white spaniel, and a new house in the suburbs, with wonderful neighbors; life could not get much better!

CHAPTER 13

Radar for Identifying the Abused in the Classroom

Trust your hunches. They're usually based on facts filed away just below the conscious level.

—Dr. Joyce Brothers

IRONICALLY, OR 'GODICALLY', I began my career, eventually teaching the very ages where I myself experienced some of my biggest pain and most of my rejection. Yes, I identified child abuse in my students. Yes, I reported it. I never tolerated bullying.

One of the ironies of my teaching career is that I had a radar for knowing which student in my class was most likely being molested. At the time, however, if you had asked me if I myself was a victim of sexual abuse, I would have said no.

My first instance was back in California during my second year of teaching. I had a little first grader who was naughty. I can't recall the exact issue that day, but I had made her sit by herself so she would not bother her peers. When I finally had a moment alone

44

with her, I point blank asked her if she had a 'touching problem.' We had implemented a new curriculum about abuse. The curriculum emphasized one's skin was a boundary for each person's body and that there were 'good' touches, like a hug from mom, and 'bad' touches, like hitting. The curriculum taught that there was a kind of touch that might make a person feel uncomfortable, like if someone touched the part of your body covered by a swimsuit.

She answered that she had a problem, and with her first grade words, told what had been happening since her mother had begun a new nighttime job. I explained that I would get her help to make the situation stop. I immediately reported the incident and forty minutes later she was called from the classroom never to return.

Embarrassed, scared, and trapped was how I felt when her mother came running into the classroom at the end of the day in search of her child, who had never made it off the bus. Never in my wildest dreams did I think I would be the one to have to look that mother in the eye, and tell her what I had done. That, because of my report, her husband, who had done the unimaginable, was being arrested and that her daughter would not sleep at home that night. Luckily, this little girl's story was believed, and she had support and counseling; her father pled guilty so that his little girl would not have to testify against him in court.

The second time I reported, it did not go so well. I was teaching second grade that year. I had my own little bookworm in my class. A student was reading, rather than participating in my exciting lessons? It made me curious. Now I was receiving the same book-hidden-in-the-math-text treatment, which I had dished out to my teacher.

This student was under a doctor's care for bladder infections and would pee her pants in class daily. She had other 'accidents,' as well. Frustrated beyond words, I tried to solve the problem by allowing any bathroom time needed, whenever, for however long, with no teacher permission required. Nothing worked. Cleaning up this daily mess was not something I was trained to handle in a normal classroom situation. I finally point blank asked her if she had a problem with touching.

She explained that her stepfather was abusing her. Without going into all the details, the detective and social services decided that the times she said the incidences had occurred, did not line up with the times her mother had left her alone with her step father, so they dropped the case and decided she was lying. She had no support and was now known to her family as 'the daughter who peed and pooped her pants, and made up huge lies about her stepfather and child abuse'.

I was in trouble for filing a false report. The parents hated me. Huge blue eyes welling with tears are seared in my memory from when I told her I still believed her story.

Years later, I received a letter from her mother. She shared that she had found Christ and felt compelled to share with and thank me. Her now college-aged daughter was in therapy and that my report had finally been corroborated a few years later when her husband went on to abuse their biological daughter.

Teachers say, "There is something not right there," and "Something is going on," which are euphemisms for suspected child abuse. We all have students that, if we had to pick one, would bet it had happened to or might be at risk for sexual abuse in the future.

Each year, all teachers and students in the public school system are required to view videos on childhood abuse, including sexual abuse. Teachers are mandated reporters, yet what I did; point blank asking a child if they were being molested is not protocol. We are not to ask. The reason given is that we are not trained and therefore might elicit false reports, or goad them into agreeing with our accusations, though they may be false. Unfortunately, this is one factor why the stepfather got off in the above example.

It is a lose-lose-lose situation. Teachers can't ask. Students are supposed to confide to an adult, like a counselor, who they most likely do not have a close relationship with. And in some areas, the foster care situation is so bad there is fear of further abuse happening if a report is filed, validated, and the child is placed in the system.

CHAPTER 14

Living for Perfection, The Perfect Princess

Come to me all you weary and burdened and I will give you rest. Take my yoke upon you and learn from me; for I am gentle and humble in heart, and you will find rest for your souls.

—*Matthew 11:28-29*

FULL, BUT EXHAUSTING WAS a good description of my life during this time. From the outside, it seemed I could do it all. I believed I could too. My home was spotless at all times and each Saturday was devoted to deep cleaning it top to bottom. Dinners were home-cooked meals, complete with meat, two veggies, rolls, and dessert. The children were clean and shiny and expected to be 'A' students. Daily exercise was a part of my day. I was also sometimes, not so secretly judgmental, of those who did not measure up.

The trouble was I had very few perfect days, 'perfect' being the key word. My perfect day would be up early, children dressed, and fed; off to school, and teaching we would go. Teach twenty second graders and, do it with zest and joy, ending the day by completing all tasks, planning, grading, and parental phone calls. Take a quick run before grabbing the kids, (gotta keep the weight down), then a big breath, having made it through the day, exhausted. Time for my real job, the most important one, I would think. Smile! Pick the kids up. Talk about our day. Homework. Play time. Dinner. Story-time. Kisses. There were very few nights as I closed my eyes to sleep that I felt satisfied, that I had met my own very high standards. I was never happy.

I don't believe that what I have described above is just a result of abuse and my desire to have control and create feelings of value; I think we are all trying to prove our value. Men, women, and children, we are always being evaluated and compared with one another. Was what we just did good enough? Was it the BEST? Could it be improved? We live in a competitive world where the message is always, who is the best? Prettiest? Fastest? Thinnest? Fittest? Richest? Smartest? Everyone is striving to compete.

There was one reoccurring issue in our marriage; I would pick the same fight over and over again. Every month or so, I would cry and tell my husband I did not 'feel' loved. There was always something he wasn't doing to make me happy. He wasn't talking to me enough. We weren't going on enough dates. He was spending too much time in his office paying bills, or golfing, or caring for the lawn. He would listen, apologize, and then try harder. The poor guy was in a losing battle because no matter what he said or did, it would never be enough to satisfy my thirst for reassurance. I did not believe I was worthy of love, so there was nothing he could ever do to fill that hole. I made it his responsibility for me to be okay.

Because of this drive for perfection, I would bounce back and forth between teaching full time, staying home, and then back to part time, trying to find balance. Jeff just wanted me to be happy, anything to make me happy, but my issues were bigger than a job. I was searching for worth.

CHAPTER 15

Dad Follows Christ

If a man has a hundred sheep, and one of them goes astray,
does he not leave the ninety-nine and go to the mountains
to seek the one that is straying?

—*Matthew 18:12*

MEANWHILE, MY FATHER HAD progressed to his third wife. Along the way, something miraculous had happen. Dad came to faith in Jesus. He, a believer in reincarnation, had visited a church for the first time in 30 years, and as soon as he sat down, he began to weep.

I remember as a little girl having reincarnation explained to me when I tried to share Jesus with my father. While never outright mocked, the implication was that Christians were not very smart, nor highly educated. It was inferred... Christianity was for the dumb. I don't know why his beliefs never shook me. I knew, even at nine years old when I would pray and cry out to God for him, that he was the blinded one. Now, with his new found faith, I was skeptical waiting to see if Christianity would stick. He became a changed man.

Surprised disbelief, as well as irritation describe my feelings during his journey toward Salvation. I was so happy that my dad had discovered Jesus; he had faith. He seemed to be behaving and reacting differently, better differently. He was so thrilled with his new found discovery of Jesus. It was as if he had discovered sunshine and rainbows.

But, *now*, he was worried about *my* salvation. I did not appreciate the irony of his concern when I had been a Christian for years. Dad would share his passion and his exploits in Christianity and it did not make me want to draw closer to God. Instead, it made me feel like a failure and that I could never measure up to being his type of Christian.

My dad was not just a Christian; he was a 'Super Christian.' Need a Bible Study leader? He was on it. Need a volunteer to pray over all 300 seats before services each Sunday? He was your guy. Need someone to speak and give his testimony? Name the day. He seemed to be working on his Christianity just like he worked to conquer karate to become a black belt, or the years spent learning bridge to become a master player. I could never put my finger on what felt so distasteful about his version of Christianity. I now know that he was *working* for God's love and not receiving the unconditional grace He freely offers. He had yet to receive the understanding of his identity as God's son

His newfound faith began to work on his inner core. When my son, my first child, was a baby, my father dropped in to visit. We sat outside on the grass with the baby on a blanket between us. My Father told me he was deeply sorry for 'all he had done,' yet mentioned no specifics and asked for my forgiveness.

I thought at the time he was apologizing for being a jerk of a Dad. Some of my bitterness welled up and memories flashed through my mind; him leaving and humiliating my mother, his frugality and lack of generosity with finances. Resentment reigned when I thought about him not once attending an event where I was the star in high school. I recalled his lack of support or encouragement of my interests, like cheerleading and debate team competitions. I'll never forget the strangest of all, there was a peculiar sensation, a bubbling in my brain and a buzzing in my ears like my thoughts were being sucked into a vortex, a tunnel or direction I did not want to go. Immediately, a wall went up in my mind.

There was silence between us, a long protracted period of waiting for my reply. I had been taught that it takes a lot of courage for a person to say, "I am sorry," therefore one should always accept an apology. I couldn't do it!

I felt an iron-like wall of resistance within me. I ended up telling him that just because he was sorry and ready to be forgiven, did not mean that I was ready to receive it or forgive him. He told me I would not have peace until I accepted his remorse and forgave him. I believe now he was apologizing for the abuse, but I was still repressing and/or suppressing it, and did not, or was not willing, to remember it.

they faced one another with a large flat piece of furniture between them, similar to a dining room buffet in shape. Their heads were bowed in reverence and above their heads they had huge crossed wings that arched above their bent heads and above the surface of the furniture. As I looked toward them, a glowing light began to illuminate and became brighter and brighter, radiating within the center of the arch wings. I heard a voice say, "This is the Lord."

I replied, "I want to see the Lord!"

Slowing, I looked upward from the glowing base up, up, and up to what would have been the face and 'whoosh,' I was swept away by the two angels that had brought me. With an angel holding each out-stretched arm, back we flew back through the dimensions, over the continents, over the United States and like a magnetic paper doll, my spirit snapped back into my body. I let out a huge breath of air, and awoke.

The next day, I shared my dream with a devoted friend and neighbor. She told me I was describing the Holy of Holies and the cherubim who worship with the Ark of the Covenant between them. What? She even had an artist's rendition of what that might look like and showed me scripture about it from the Bible.

> *17 "Make an atonement cover of pure gold—two and a half cubits long and a cubit and a half wide. 18 And make two cherubim out of hammered gold at the ends of the cover. 19 Make one cherub on one end and the second cherub on the other; make the cherubim of one piece with the cover, at the two ends. 20 The cherubim are to have their wings spread upward, overshadowing the cover with them. The cherubim are to face each other, looking toward the cover.*
> *—Exodus 25: 17-20, NIV*

I was in awe. I had never heard of the Holy of Holies, the Ark of the Covenant, or cherubim. I had never read this in the Bible. More than anything I was thrilled that God was teaching me, even as I slept. I remember telling her the picture she had was similar, but the cherubim looked different.

I learned a lot about prayer just three doors down the street. I can't remember what the gathering of Christian women was studying, but I do remember the prayer. When we prayed together, our prayers were answered. I began to embrace prayer and wanted to learn how to talk to God. I was like a sponge soaking up everything the women said.

The bottom line of all of this is God really, really, *really* wants us to pray. Prayer is our channel of communication to Him, our key to intimacy with Him, and the conduit by which we receive all of the love, affection, and gifts he has for us.

I have heard Christians talk a lot about prayer, like there is this magical formula to get God to give you what you want. A few use the word 'Faith,' like a cure-all. God did not give you what you asked for because, "You did not have enough faith." I have witnessed believers avoid doctors and reject medical treatment as a common practice, because to receive treatment would be a lack of 'faith.'

Time and again, I myself have given the God of the universe his marching orders. Some say prayer is about trying to be Holy. Some say fasting is the key to getting God to listen to you so that you will have power in prayer. I have tried everything that well meaning Christians have suggested I do to get closer to God. But I come back again and again to my dream, "You go there when you pray."

When we pray, we go before the very throne of God and speak

to him from our hearts. It is not about being holy enough or by our own efforts. The whole point of our very creation is about forming relationships, including and especially, a God relationship. Jesus has made us worthy as we surrender to this journey we call Christianity.

There was much I learned from the prayer down the street, but I took everything said to heart. Obedience? What did God want? Just tell me and I would do it. Service? I'm your girl! Need a meal brought to the sick? I'll bring it to them, even if I have never met them. In my need to control and please, I fell easily into works. In order to save everyone else from shared trauma and abuse, I became the buffer and the hyper vigilant soldier of service. Like my Dad, I became 'Super Christian.'

I became a bit goofy – weird, even. I was looking forward to sharing what I was discovering about Jesus with somebody, anybody. Occasionally, I would approach strangers and talk about God. I began attending a Charismatic Church. I loved the freedom and the power of God there, but I didn't know enough to be able to discern truth from error.

I had become 'religious.' I now cringe when I think about it. My definition of religion is believing that positive Christian practices such as giving, praying, Bible reading, evangelizing, or attending services makes God love you more than he already does. It is the hidden belief that not only does God love you because of this; but also, that you are spiritually superior to a person who does not implement the above Christian practices.

A hunger for knowledge was growing in me. So much goodness and many wondrous experiences were occurring, and yet, there was something off in my understanding and the belief system I had about Jesus, as well as my beliefs about myself.

I think the root of this performance for God was my desire to use religion to make myself worthy. If I could just do Christianity right, then maybe I would feel holy and loveable. Maybe the underlying sense of shame would be erased.

CHAPTER 18

The Revelation

Awake, awake, ... clothe yourself with strength. Put on your garments of splendor... The uncircumcised and defiled will not enter you again, Shake off your dust; rise up; sit enthroned...free yourself from the chains on your neck, O captive Daughter of Zion. For this is what the Lord says: You were sold for nothing, and you will be redeemed without money.

—Isaiah 52:1-3

JANUARY 12, 2000, I still remember the day. We were celebrating my dear friend Cheryl's birthday when we got on the subject of my past. We discussed some of the weird things my father had done, and that I had vaguely wondered if I was ever abused. When she asked why I wondered, I told her that my father was into weird things sexually, and that I had often seen him nude, even as a teenager. Pornography was available to us kids and he told us inappropriate sexual stories about his past sexual escapades.

Pornography, available to children, and inappropriate nudity alone could be considered sexual abuse; nevertheless, stories of sexual conquests were another level of abuse and inappropriate exposure. I had an 'Ah ha' moment when Cheryl told me those things were not normal, were inappropriate, and took away a child's innocence. As we prayed, we asked for revelation if there was abuse; little did I know what was coming.

A nightmare entangled me. I was choking. Something was stopping me from being able to breathe. Was I being strangled? Was something blocking my airway? It felt like I was being attacked and could not get the invisible claws to release my throat. Terrified, I awoke trying to catch my breath, crying out to Jesus.

Next in my sleep, two huge angels came to me and stood on either side of me. I was a little girl again, sitting in the chrome dinette chair of the studio apartment. The coin was in my father's palm, held in front of my eyes swaying back and forth, back and forth. A metal choke collar surrounded my neck and, my left leg was shackled to the leg of the table with a prison chain and ankle cuff. The angel asked me if I wanted to be set free. I said yes. The angel took a key and unlocked the collar and cuff, and the chains fell to the ground. Immediately, as the chains fell, I sat up in the bed fully awake. Now I remembered.

CHAPTER 19

The Telling

For nothing is hidden that will not be revealed, nor anything
secret, that will not be known and come into the light.
—Luke 8:17

THAT MORNING, AFTER THE children were gone to school,
I told my husband what I had experienced. As I began to tell him
about my dream and what had come to my consciousness, I began
to shake and quiver and tremor. My body trembled as I stuttered
and wailed, trying to get the words out. The sound was a high-
pitched keening from a deep unknown place within my center.
Never before or since, have I experienced those physical sensations
or cried in that way. Jeff held me and rocked me and wiped my
tears as I began to process my first memories. That was the first day
of grief. I remember having some time alone and crying like Jesus
did to his father, "Father, Father, why have you forsaken me?" As
I cried, I felt a double dose of grief; grief that my father sexually
molested me and grief that my Father in Heaven had allowed it.

We decided that I needed to share my realization with my family.

As I began to go to the basement to use another phone for privacy, Jeff asked where I was going. Couldn't he be with me? "Don't you trust me?" he asked. I remember the dawning of understanding of an inner truth coming to the light. I lowered my eyes and shook my head, "No, I don't trust anybody," I replied to my husband of twelve years. He asked to be with me, anyway, and he held me as I wailed through the story to my disbelieving mother.

Next it was time to tell my brothers. Shocked and disbelieving was the response. I reminded them of our shared background and our experiences. They pretty much confirmed the timing of things: Dad's strangeness, the pornography, and the sexual inappropriateness. I felt supported to the degree that they 'said' they believed me and that they were sorry it happened. No one ever called me a liar, but there was not necessarily support either.

Up to this point, I had always been the lynch pin of the family, the rock. The good, the bad and the ugly; no topic had been off limits in our home. My family has always been very upfront about what was really going on in our lives, but I was the one who would keep the rest of the family in the loop of each other's happenings.

Phoning my siblings and my mother, I apologized in advance. In the coming weeks, I was not going to be able to be there for them because I was not okay, and, "it is okay that I am not okay."

Recognizing that I was an absolute emotional mess, and giving myself permission to be the train wreck that I was, was a huge first step in healing my perfectionism and striving.

"I am not Okay and it is Okay that I am not Okay"

For the first time I was able to express what had been true for 30 years. I was not Okay. Being molested by my dad was not Okay. Keeping silent and pretending all was well was not Okay. I had not been Okay since that summer morning in my dad's apartment. Finally, with these profound words, I began the journey of grieving, speaking, and healing.

My family said they understood. With my brothers, our communication and close relationship ended during this time. I believe that it was too painful for my family to choose to walk alongside me as I began the process of healing. They were, and are still, reluctant to let go of their ideal of their 'good' dad. There is still love between us and we have grown closer over the last few years, but I had nothing to give to them during this time.

Luckily, my mother had her revelation in church, which validated what I said. My stepfather always fully believed in my story. Having a family member say they believe you is very healing; however, it is not the same as having someone ask and want to hear what happened and how it affected you. Nobody ever asked how I was, how I was holding up, or how my counseling was going. It was a once and done as far as they were concerned. The message was clear, "Let's not talk about that."

CHAPTER 20

The Preparation

The Lord will go before you and be your rear guard.
—Isaiah 52:12

TWO PIVOTAL THINGS HAPPENED prior to my healing. First, a friend told me, "You have an inability to receive."

I was so proud of myself. I had inherited a small amount of money from a class action suit as a result of my father's death from mesothelioma. My pride was in giving my inheritance away. Jeff had told me the money was mine to do with as I wished, and I wanted to make a difference in people's lives. I searched for people in need and I gave the money to try to meet their need.

Offended when she seemed to be criticizing my giving, I thought, *how dare she? Doesn't she know how much I am pleasing God?* I did, however, ask God if I had an inability to receive, to change me.

As I look back, I understand now, that my lack of trust made me resist receiving from anyone, even God. After all, I had received that which I hated when my dad molested me. I never believed that I could receive something guilt-free, no strings attached. I did not want to owe anybody anything. I despised any inner weakness in asking for help, even to the point of walking rather than asking for a ride to pick up my car from the shop. Being the hero was my preferred role, and I disliked being the needy one. My concept of God and lack of trust was very much based on how I viewed my earthly father.

The second thing to prepare me for healing happened when I began taking medicine for depression.

I had struggled with depression for years. Fear and anxiety were often the motivating factors for my life choices and the way I parented. Finally, I decided to seek help. Increased stability and peace were the results of going on medication. Within two weeks, I was shocked at the change in how my mind and emotions were functioning. I still worried and felt both negative and positive emotions such as fear and joy, but my mind did not stay on a negative track, overwhelming me. I remember thinking, "Is this what normal feels like? Is this how normal people process life?"

As time has passed, I have had well-meaning people tell me that taking medication is a crutch, that it blocks you from feeling badly enough to force you to deal with your issues. "Bull," is my response. Unfortunately, I did not trust myself to know what I needed. I tried to come off the medication several times only to suffer. Coming to accept the gift of medication has been difficult. Christian circles sometimes view needing and using depression medicine as a weakness. I have been told that depression is unexpressed anger. Perhaps this is true, since anger is an emotion that is difficult for me to express. I have often wondered however, if researchers did a study, there might be a correlation between abuse in children and burning out your serotonin. After all, you have to pretend to be happy and okay immediately after you are hurt. Maybe that affects brain chemistry.

We who follow Christ hear that God prepares a way for us before we even know what we need. As I look back over my journey, I see this as true. So many people and encounters and seasons with different denominations, played a part in helping me unlock and heal.

From my Catholic friends, I learned and experienced a reverence and respect for God and his holiness. For a time, I hung out with Christians who would knock various denominations. We spent time discussing interpretations of Christianity and justified what we believed. *We* knew the real truth - much like politics today. The big problem we had with our Catholic brothers and sisters was going through the priest instead of directly to God. Luckily I had an experience that changed my mind.

My husband had a trip to Paris over Easter weekend. We were homeschooling our kids at the time and joined him. As we visited different churches, we observed each sacred place filled with a holy reverence; the pews were full. I still remember visiting Notre Dame on Good Friday. There was no priest, nor any kind of Mass, yet each and every seat was taken. Kneeling in silence and prayer, a holy hush filled the cathedral. I looked out over all the bowed heads and felt sorrow for wrongly judging people. I had never gone to a church to silently pray. I never honored Good Friday. For me, Easter was of course about the Resurrection of Jesus, but it almost seemed a bit of a show, with Easter Sunday often used as a time to judge the sporadic church attendees who only show up for holidays.

From my Baptist friends, I learned about Jesus, his love for us, and his desire for us to know him. Every single sermon was focused on Jesus. I learned of his love, his compassion, his goodness, and his birth and resurrection. Practices, such as prayer and scripture reading were encouraged. Service was taught. Baptists showed me love in action. Don't tell someone in crises to call you if they need something; instead take action. Bring a meal, send a gift card, mow their lawn, and clean their houses; serve one another.

Power and authority in praying is what I learned from my Charismatic friends. They pray out loud, and often place their hands on the individual they are praying for. I learned what we can ask for when we pray, and especially why God wants us to ask. God hears us and answers us.

All of these preparations played a role in my healing. Being open to receiving, taking medicine to get me through the emotional upheaval and depression, and the team of people God would bring to help made all the difference.

CHAPTER 21

My Bonnie – Her
Name is Holy

*Two are better than one, because they have a good return
for their labor: If either of them falls down; one can help
the other up. But pity anyone who falls and has no one to
help him...though one may be overpowered, two can defend
themselves. A cord of three strands is not quickly broken.*
—Ecclesiastes 4:9-15

JEFF KNEW IMMEDIATELY THAT counseling was needed to
make me better. "Honey, I have no idea how to help, but I will
support you. Just go talk to someone and get better." I had friends
who spoke highly of Bonnie, a Christian counselor.

Never have I encountered such encouragement, compassion,
and lack of judgment. We would meet weekly and slowly, through
much pain and many tears, I started to process my feelings and
emotions, and events of the past, and to truly feel better.

On our first meeting, I told Bonnie how afraid I was. I was

73

natural instinct, has had, and continues to have repercussions. There is a time, place, and age for each individual's sexuality to blossom and come to maturity. Forcing a child to participate in a sexual act affects behavior. This is why one of the indicators for abuse in children is sexual knowledge and behavior that is not age appropriate. The abuse affects one's sexuality forever.

We dealt with the "S-word", a word I hate – 'Slut,' to realize that I was acting out of my abuse and maybe, just maybe, the whole promiscuity thing was not entirely my fault, that sexually abused people act out, was a sigh of relief to me. I came to understand how my behavior was a natural result of my inner heart. When I hear the gossip about the latest local girl who has the bad reputation - the fast girl, the party girl, my heart breaks for her, and what she may have suffered. If people only knew her history, the lack of love and very likely abuse, maybe they would nurture and love, rather than judge. I have such compassion for promiscuous women. If we only knew our value, we would not give ourselves so lightly.

Dear Reader, as I continue to write, you may notice that at times my pronouns will change from first person to an inclusive form. This is by intention. I believe that my statements about Jesus and what God says about me, are for us, for all. In fact I would ask you to consider asking yourself, "If God is real and Jesus is real, would I want to know? " My hope is that you will say the prayer, "God, if you are real, will you show me?" And finally, "If there are any blocks that stop me from receiving good in my life and especially love, would you remove them?"

And, for those unraveling the trauma and courageous enough to accept the healing and receive the love God has for you, be kind to yourself, be patient, and simply ask Father. "Lord, I am ready for healing. I am ready to receive your love. Show me the way, today."

CHAPTER 22

The J-Word –
Jesus Is Not a Dirty Word

Get rid of all bitterness, rage and anger...along with every
form of malice. Be kind and compassionate with one another
forgiving each other, just as in Christ God forgave you
—Ephesians 4:31-32

THE F-WORD, THE S-WORD, The B-word, this was how my students would report on one another for cussing when I was a teacher. I soon learned to have my students whisper the actual words in my ear after discovering that "fart, stupid, and brat" were often times the words in question.

The J-word; it can be controversial. Jesus can be controversial. In fact, for some, just hearing the J-word causes a block in the heart and mind. "Him again," muttered under the breath with shaking knowing heads makes it very clear their disdain and confusion for the truth of Jesus. Not everyone embraces Him, and some will mock, but I needed saving. I needed saving from shame, rejection and fear – I needed Jesus. And He was faithful.

Authority was key. As a child, my highest authority demonstrated through words and actions, that I was worth less than his sexual impulses and gratification. The fact that a higher authority than my dad - the highest authority of all, says I am worthwhile, valuable, and precious, was needed to nullify the past. For my every weakness and pain, there is an equal and opposite strength, and healing in Jesus.

Lauren Daigle puts this so beautifully in her song, *You Say*.

I keep fighting voices in my mind that say I'm not enough...
It is easy for someone traumatized by abuse to not feel valued or enough.

Every single lie that tells me I will never measure up...
There is a constant devaluing of self; replaying the scenes and feeling defeated over and over again.

Am I more than just the sum of every high and every low?
Remind me once again just who I am, because I need to know.....
I needed constant reassurance of my identity, whose I was, who He made me to be before...

The only thing that matters now is everything You think of me
In You I find my worth, in You I find my identity, ...

These lyrics she writes in this beautiful song, poetically speaks to the heart, of the give and take provided by Jesus, and how we identify with Him. In my saving, I came to fully embrace the foundational precept of Christianity - that I am worth so much, so valuable, that God sent his son Jesus to die for me. This is and ever shall be the pivotal turning from worthless to priceless in my heart.

Four basic principles of Christianity were the key for me to get better.

I believe:

1. At salvation, Jesus comes to live inside of you and you live inside of him.

2. We do not have greater "rights" than Jesus.

3. When we surrender, we allow Jesus to do greater things than what we can accomplish with our own power.

4. We are forgiven all our past, present, and future sins.

As a Christ follower, I am forgiven my sins; all my sins, past, present and future. Believing this, and understanding the great exchange that happened on the cross, was so crucial to getting better. You might be wondering what is the big deal with Christians and forgiveness. Forgiveness is something that Jesus asks us to do. At times, it feels unjust to forgive everyone, especially abusers. Forgiving removes hatred and bitterness within the forgiver, something that is good for us. I had a lot of forgiving to do. I'm not sure which was the bigger task of forgiveness - forgiving my father or forgiving myself.

My fantasy, in the reel of my mind's eye, was me kicking my father as hard as I could in the chest as I screamed, "NOOOOOO!" thus stopping the abuse. In my imagining, the force of my ten-year-old legs is so strong that it breaks my dad's ribs as he goes flying across the room, smashing against the wall. I hated myself for not kicking, for not stopping him.

You might be thinking, "What do you mean forgiving yourself? You're the victim here." I had to forgive myself the blame and false responsibility as well as the self-hatred. The self-blame, hatred, and guilt we put on our child selves are the biggest hindrances we have to living a life of joy.

Just the way a parent is upset when their children are picked on, or are blamed for something they did not do, so is the case with God. The way I beat up myself was something I needed to apologize for. Weird, I know, but true. Also, by forgiving myself, I could begin to love myself.

Forgiving my dad was hard, very hard. My forgiveness became an act of faith. It didn't *feel* as if I forgave him. I made a choice. I would not allow bitterness to consume me. Even so, I would feel anger, and the bitterness would rise within me. I would tell myself that since Jesus forgave me, I choose to forgive, too. I had to finally be gut wrenchingly honest with Jesus and tell him I just couldn't do it. The most powerful part of this was surrender. Through this dilemma, this conflict, I refused to fake it and pretend I wasn't struggling, or to paste my Christian smile on my face and say, "Oh life is rosy, and the birds are singing and I forgive." I learned something so profound. I told Jesus I was weak, but that He lives in me, so I give up. If he wanted me to forgive my dad, I surrender my heart, and my mind, and my body to Him. He would have to come do it. Basically, I can't, but you can, in, and through me.

Somehow through this surrender, and my desire to forgive, I can honestly say that it has happened. Somehow, I am able to separate my good dad, the dad that will live forever, the friend and confidant, the quarterback of my touchdowns, from the abuser. I sometimes talk to him. I know he is sorry, and proud of me.

Self-pity is something I had to battle. For a while, all I could see within myself was the poor little abused girl, the poor little victim. As my mind healed, I received the truth of who God says I am, no longer a victim.

It is easy as you read this to get caught up in the bad parts and to feel pity for abuse survivors. It is ironic that we were victims, but we are not victims. We are survivors, but more than survivors, we are conquerors.

As I have been led to begin talking about this most taboo subject of incest, the most common and well-meaning comments are, "I am so sorry this happened to you." I have been able to receive and hear it in the manner that it is intended, yet I always have hated hearing this. It feels like pity. No one wants to be pitied. The comments that have sung within my heart are, "You are strong and courageous. Look at all you have gone through and what you have accomplished." These words are so very affirming for those who have painful pasts.

Giving up my rights was another portion of my healing. Being the basket case I was for a few years, not everyone validated or agreed with me. I had to give up my right to receive apologies, my right to be validated, and my right to be understood. Jesus was not liked. He was not validated. He was not understood. Why should we think we deserve all of the above? Identifying with Jesus and these parts of his Cross were crucial in becoming my real self.

I choose to forgive whether I get an apology or not. So many times I have held onto anger because I did not get my, "I'm sorry." Or worse yet, their tone was not very remorseful, so they did not really mean it, even though they had said it! I have found that for me to pray for good things to occur in my 'enemy's' life, helps me to actually forgive and feel it. My favorite forgiveness prayer is, "May they know how much you love them. May they know you delight in, and are, for them. May they come to know you better." There is something about truly wishing someone well that helps us to let go of bitterness.

The desires to be validated and understood go hand in hand. We feel the way we feel, believe the way we believe, and often want others to see our side to confirm we are right. These desires are neither good nor bad. It is awesome when someone 'gets' you, agrees with you, confirms that you are smart, and validates you.

I wanted so much to be liked, that I was angry or crushed if someone did not see life the way that I do. Rejection and that same old rejection song would begin to play if someone did not 'get' me. Even worse, I am an expert at reading a situation and can become chameleon-like to get people to like me. How could I be my authentic self if my overriding desire was to be liked?

Letting go of people pleasing has been a challenge. I began to learn that Jesus likes me, and more so, he is not trying to change and improve me. It has been eye opening that the way I glorify Him is by being true to myself. This means being honest about my emotions, physical needs, and in my relationships. Much of my forgiveness of myself was because I almost felt that disappointing people was a sin. Jesus began to teach me how to trust my instincts and desires and to detach from the false guilt I felt when I no longer rushed to make everyone happy.

CHAPTER 23

Sexual Intimacy

I belong to my beloved and his desire is for me.
—Song of Songs 7:10

WE'VE HEARD THE CODE words, the spelled words, the hints and innuendos between the adults, as we listened in as children. We suspect. There is something that adults know that we children are not to understand. We've seen the broadcasts. "Oh gross, kissing on TV," we may have giggled. As young teens, we might have practiced kissing our own arm. Most of us have seen every enactment, from tender first kisses to violent rapes as we have watched movies from our television sets. Some of us have even viewed pornography, whether from curiosity, for self-stimulation, or by accident as we stumbled through the Internet. There is a mystique to it all, and yet a universal knowledge that the sex drive and procreation are a part of life, in fact, brings forth life. It is one of the greatest forces on earth.

I don't know if I am normal. I admit to all of the above, but have always wondered.

Should I have rules to my sexuality? Are there boundaries that are God given? Maybe God has 'dos and don'ts' for us when it comes to sex. Is my husband happy with our love life? Is God? Am I really free to express love unashamed? These are all questions I have asked and struggle with.

It seems to me that men are more sexually 'free' than women are in that they don't get so hung up on what is right or wrong when it comes to sex. They seem more visually, as well as physically driven, and sexuality does not affect a man's mind in the same way it affects a woman's. Not to say that men do not ever struggle with guilt or shame, just that they do not seem to think about it as much.

Before I began my 'religious' journey of trying to please God, and before I remembered the abuse of my childhood, my husband and I enjoyed the joys of marital intimacy. I did not give much thought to what was going on in my mind during our times together. I was usually in the moment and did not experience much guilt or shame. When I drew closer to God, and wanting to please him in every way, I began to struggle.

Later, as I remembered the abuse, our intimate life suddenly became very complicated. Before I was with Jeff, even with my wild ways, I was never able to fully enjoy sexual intimacy. Looking back, I believe it was a matter of trust and not being able to give over control to another person. After our marriage though, oohlala! We were compatible and enjoyed our alone time. But now, the devastating memories and shame threatened to destroy it all.

Little did I suspect how God would use all the pain to bring a greater understanding of love. Time and again, God would illuminate the parallel between the love he was showing me, the fight he was waging on my behalf, with the love and fight Jeff was waging for me, for us, and for our family. Jeff was my champion.

Usually it is the women who battle for the communication and verbal intimacy in a relationship. When things are not right between couples, the women bring it up. This time though, Jeff was willing to go 'there.' He would be the initiator, calling me out on my withdrawal, my shutting down, and trying to shut him out. He pursued me, but not sexually this time. He would ask me to talk, to process my thoughts and pain with him. Before this, I had always wondered if I didn't pursue truth, honesty and intimacy in our communication, would we even have any as a couple, because my husband certainly wasn't going to bring it up.

My understanding prince of a husband communicated. He asked me to tell him if there were any particular things he did that triggered memories. There were a few specific things, which he was careful to avoid.

My most healing moment with Jeff happened one night as the candles were lit and the children were asleep. He asked how he could help me, and I told him that I needed for him to love me, kiss me, yet to take nothing from me. I needed him to forego his need and desire for me. Call it naked cuddling if you will, but I had never had a man forego his desire for me, to sacrifice for me, and to just be held. As we embraced in the candlelight, it was as though a balm of healing was radiating from him into my soul.

Often though, the struggle continued in my mind. No longer was I carefree, but now I felt that lovemaking was shameful. I knew, logically, that it was not the case, but I felt full of shame when we were intimate. I was like a tennis line judge, and my mind was narrating a play-by-play, with side line judges scoring each thought, each kiss, each position of the 'ok' or 'not ok' side. Was this evil? Was this okay? Was this something my dad did to me?

I battled…

Focus! I chastised myself with intensity. *Be in the moment! Think about Jeff. Think about your love.*

Flash! **Visual of the Abuse.** *Did Dad do that?*

Do. Not. Think. Of. That.

Oh God stop it! Please. Help me!

It was a silent movie on a continuous reel showing the highlights of what I did not want to remember.

Because of the struggle in my mind, I sought understanding and came to some personal, as well as universally held Christian convictions, regarding sexual intimacy.

- Sex is God's idea. He, to produce life and *pleasure*, created it.
- Sex is ordained for marriage.
- God wants his couples to be able to be naked and unashamed when they are together.
- The marriage bed is undefiled. (Both a command and an impartation.)
- My personal boundaries are good and right because they are what I choose.
- Sex should not involve pain.
- We are free when it comes to marital intimacy.

My dream for my sexual healing was the desire to be fully present with my husband as we enjoyed one another with no present or after effects of shame. I wanted to be able to be in the moment, not in my head battling and evaluating my thoughts. I did not want memories, or pornography to be part of our time together. Lofty goals perhaps, but it was what I wanted and what I thought God wanted.

At first, the way I dealt with the sexual intimacy was through prayer. Before we would make love, I would pray in my heart that

God would allow me to enjoy my time with my husband with no shame. I would remind him that he said that our union was good, and ask him to guard my mind. I would bind a spirit of shame in the name of Jesus and tell it that it had no place in our marriage bed. If a memory would occur, I would silently tell it to go away in the name of Jesus. Instantly, it would be gone and not come back during our time together.

I wish I could say that in a few weeks, all was well, but this was not the case. As a few years passed, my prayers changed. I would ask God to help me to embrace my sexuality; that it was God-given. With this prayer I had even more freedom and fewer attacks.

Today, I have come to the point, where I wonder if I will ever be completely free from all sexual shame. Will there come a time, I don't have to pray before lovemaking? I always love and enjoy my intimate time but there is still the occasional battle. A nameless heaviness can descend. It feels like an attack. This may always be a tender place, a place where I can love myself, accepting that the consequences of the sin of abuse is long lasting. I refuse to let it ruin my God-given right to love, and intimacy with my husband.

Most recently, I have embraced my inner 'I,' the ownership of my sexuality. I think to myself, *I like, I want, I prefer, I desire.* This has enabled me to stay in the moment and has provided me more freedom and enjoyment than I had ever hoped. My sexuality was stolen from me and tainted with shame. It has taken me 45 years to embrace this God-given gift of human sexuality. Part of my creation is as a sexual being. I now own it and enjoy it. Jeff's pretty happy too!!

CHAPTER 24

Grace, Our Righteousness

Chris' definition of Grace: 1) Being let off the hook for a negative act even though you deserve a consequence. 2) The power of goodness greater than you can understand working on your behalf. 3) Jesus.

THIS STRUGGLE FOR SEXUAL freedom was another impetus toward embracing my authentic self. I wanted to have the freedom promised me with Salvation; freedom to accept myself and my unique wants, and most of all, the freedom to receive and embrace my worth. Yearning for freedom provoked some deep introspective questions. Why do I have value? What is unconditional love? Can humans truly give unconditional love?

The parental relationship is supposed to be the picture of unconditional love, but my picture was skewed, so how could I figure out my worth? This question made me look deep into my faith as I searched for answers.

When I studied the teachings of Jesus, and the meaning of biblical grace, I discovered that Jesus did not focus on sin and especially not sexual sin. In fact, other than his hatred of divorce and adultery, Jesus is silent on sex. The apostle Paul is more specific on sexual sins, but during Jesus' time on earth, He, Himself, was silent. Of course, we avoid lust and sexual immorality, but the nitty-gritty of sexual acts was never his focus. His focus was on love and bringing us to His perfect Father, the Father of Love.

When He was critical, it was not against the acts of the common people of His time, rather, His focus was criticizing the Pharisees, the religious leaders who were thought to have their act together. These would be the so-called 'super Christians' of their time. He would basically take their hundreds of laws, which the leaders felt that they themselves had fulfilled, and he would raise the bar higher. The Pharisees were about following the letter of the law, but often not the heart of the law.

We all pretty much can agree what sin is; stuff we do that is wrong. We could give a ten year old a 'sin' quiz and they would pretty much be able to classify sin as the following; Lying? "Yep." Stealing? "Yep." Backstabbing? "Yep." Being mean? "Yep."

As far as I know, every religion is based on the 'good' versus 'evil' paradigm. Basically, it is, I do good things, I try to be a good person, I obey the law and I avoid evil, thus I am owed: 1) God's favor and rewards, 2) Heaven, and 3) forgiveness and eternal life.

When I truly began to understand Grace and what Jesus accomplished on the cross, it blew away all of my confusion about other religions. Christianity is not based on good works. In fact, working your way into Heaven is detestable to God. It is the only religion that eliminates the great balance scale in the sky.

What I discovered with Grace is, not only does God want you to avoid sin, but performing to erase your shame, performing to earn your way to heaven, or to earn his favor, is not his desire either. Instead, he wants us to simply receive His Righteousness. My error - and it was a doozy, was only looking at God through the eyes of the Old Testament.

I did not believe it at first when my friend taught me there was a division between the Old and New Testament. Sacrilege! Is what I thought when my 'Grace' friend, Cheryl, shared this with me. She said I was combining all of the scriptures together as though they were all written to me. After all, they are all bound in the same book, right?

It took a while to decide whether or not to believe that there was a difference between the two and it just wasn't all 'in the Bible' with equal weight and meaning. I finally came to the conclusion that yes, there is a difference.

Just from a historical perspective, the New Testament was not even written until after Jesus' resurrection. Christianity began without any scriptures, just the stories of Jesus passed down from witnesses of his time on earth and the movement of the Holy Spirit. The New Testament did not even exist when Jesus was alive. They were written several decades after his death and resurrection. Later, religious leaders decided to combine the two, calling it the Old and New, and placing it all together in the Bible as one book. No wonder I was confused.

Old Testament = Judgment New Testament = Grace.

The Old Testament was the book for the Jews. The Old Testament was about religious laws, and what constitutes goodness and holiness from the eyes of a perfect God. The New Testament is about Jesus, the Savior of the world, who *provides* the perfection and holiness required by a perfect God in our stead. He brings us close to the Father through Faith in Him and nothing else.

The Old Testament had 613 laws. Much of it is full of wisdom that is practiced even today, such as crop rotation and allowing the soil to rest every seven years. There were sanitary commands, practices that have since been proved to be beneficial by science. These 613 laws range from commands on 'big sins,' like thou shall not kill, and thou shall not commit adultery, to obscure laws, like not eating dairy and meat at the same time, (adios cheeseburgers), and not sacrificing an animal with damaged testicles.

Jesus fulfilled all 613 laws. When He would preach, often speaking to the Pharisees about the law, He always did so in a way that would confront their hypocrisy. He was basically saying, "You hold yourself up as an example as one who is holy, who pleases God," and then He would up the ante.

Matthew 5: 17-48 illustrates this as Jesus teaches (Paraphrased):

"You say you don't murder. If you even think about it when angry with your brother, you are guilty. You think you don't commit adultery, but if you even look at a woman in a lustful way, you have committed adultery in your heart."

Because the Old Testament was written before the ushering in of Grace, (Jesus' ascension), many of the stories are lessons about judgment and the consequences of sin.

At this time, I had no discernment and was often terrified as I read the Old Testament. Many of the teachings from the Old Testament were like hooks that would catch my guilty heart. I felt so defective, like all those 'Woe to you,' verses were meant for me. I would identify with the sinful characters and become afraid that I would receive the same consequences they received - especially since I had the same behavior. *Yikes!*

My biggest hang up was on the word 'righteousness.' In the Old Testament, the form of doing right is mostly used, for example, one was to follow the 613 right and just moral laws set forth by God. In the New Testament, righteousness is a different form. It means the quality of being morally right or justified, free from the guilt of sin. The first form is an action, while the second form is a state of being, an impartation that happens at Salvation.

I no longer do right to 'become right' with God. Instead, I know I am operating under this new form of righteousness, which is an impartation I received at Salvation, and not something I have to do to earn. God sees me as right, not wrong. I am good. I am holy. I am a saint. I am free. I am free to choose anything I want, even to sin, and God will still - and does still, have the same love for me. These were some great answers for my big questions. He sees me as worthy and valuable, His perfect little child.

I discovered the truly good news, that righteousness is a spiritual birth that cannot be undone. God, my father, will always see me through the eyes of the perfection of Jesus. Understanding and living from this truth was not easily done as so many of my choices were made to create feelings of value.

My heart told me I was valuable when I had success. I am valuable because I do such and such, fill in the blank_____. Surprisingly, this caused me to begin a journey of quitting. I stopped trying to do right to become righteous, and to please God more.

For a period of time, I basically quit everything as far as Christian practices go - church attendance, tithing, teaching Sunday School, cooking for the church, disciplined daily Bible reading, regular prayer and quiet time; all of it; I quit. I did not quit it all on the same day, (lol), but I did end up dropping each of these practices for periods of time, some of them long periods of time. I was scared to death each time I let something go.

Was God really calling for me to drop (fill in the blank)
_____.

Impossible. All of the above are so 'good.' Aren't these the things that make us 'good Christians?' For me, all of these things were tainted. I did them all to try to mitigate my shame, to feel good about myself, to make God happy, and to earn His love. (As well as pleasing others within the church. They were all acts of doing right)

Instead, slowly, ever so slowly, I began to do right because I was right. There has been a 'sinking-in' phase for several years, which I will talk about later. But me, unloved, unworthy, abandoned, and used, already pleases God! In fact I could and cannot do anything to get him to love me, or even like me, more than he already does. Performing my heart out to earn acceptance and love was not going to get God to love me or be pleased with me any more than He was already. Allowing that to saturate my heart brought about behavior that is 'good,' loving, and kind, but not from 'trying,' but out of 'being.'

With this revelation I quit 'trying to be' a Christian. I was worn out and exhausted. I failed being good enough, I always ended up sinning. I was done with self-examination. The scripture I clung to was that I was 'perfect being made perfect,' which is in the book of Hebrews. I liken it to the comparison I have heard of two oak trees. Which is a more perfect oak tree - a tiny, baby oak tree or a full-grown majestic oak? ...They are both perfect oak trees.

As a former perfectionist, this was such good news! I am perfect right now in this very moment. Will I change, mature, and become more loving over time, especially as I receive God's love? Perhaps; I think so. It is my heart's desire, but *I* can't make it so.

CHAPTER 25

Receiving

Delight yourself in the Lord and he will give you the desire of your heart.

—Psalm 37:4

THE SECRET TO CHANGE I discovered was not in trying. It was in receiving. Receiving is so hard because we were tricked when we were abused. We somehow got ourselves into a situation where someone we trusted took advantage of us. We "received" that which we hated. Since then it has been impossible to receive and trust good gifts. Where is the catch? Where is the condition or the payback? Thus we are hesitant or unable to receive.

Love thy neighbor as you love yourself. How can we give our neighbors love if we have little love for ourselves? The process of receiving and surrendering to God's love allowed a gentleness, kindness, and tenderness toward myself to develop. I began to look back at my little kid self with different eyes. The more I allowed God to let me off the hook of performance because of his Grace, the more gracious and accepting I became with my own family.

The more I became authentically whole, the more I allowed those I loved to be their real selves. I realized I was very hard on and judgmental of others, just like I was of myself. The more it worked into my mind and heart how loving, kind and accepted I was, the easier it was to not sin. Not from trying, but just from feeling that sense of inner happiness and love. Think about it... when you are full of joy and love, do you sin? I don't think so...I believe that when you are full of love it is impossible to sin.

God began to take me on the journey of desire. Could I trust my heart? Could I trust that my desires were/are good? If I gave up the false desire of making everyone, including God happy, would I eventually *want* to pray, *want* to serve, *want* to read my Bible, *want* to give money to the needy? I wasn't sure I would, but I have found that the answer is 'yes.' I do all of the above now out of 'want' rather than 'have to,' and I believe, God has lead me on the journey of it all.

CHAPTER 26

The Battle

*We demolish arguments and every pretension that sets itself
up against the knowledge of God, and we take captive every
thought to make it obedient to Christ.*
—*2 Corinthians 10:5*

I WISH, OH HOW I wish, the Charismatic cure had worked for
me. In the beginning, I received the laying on of hands and prayers
many, many times. We prayed I would never ever remember the
abuse. We prayed that the shame would be removed from me in
the name of Jesus and never would the feelings return. I know
God could have done in an instant what has taken years to resolve.
Unfortunately, though I would have relief for a time, my troubles
would return. I know some would say I did not have enough faith.
Perhaps this is so, but for me, the problem lay in my mind.

Enter during this time, my dear friend Cheryl. Cheryl had been
through her own Journey of Grace. She had been on the quitting
journey ahead of me. God had given her eyes to read the Bible
and understand it through a lens unlike those I had encountered

in Church. She was on a discovery of codependency and setting boundaries, as well as choosing to believe what God said about her as the truth.

We would hang out and pray together. Almost weekly, we would share what was going on in each other's lives, and the lives of our families. Our conversations were refreshing drinks of water to a parched throat. The plastic smiles cracked and the masks fell to the ground, as we shared our real journey. We no longer pretended to wave our magic Christian wands and infer that we had it all together. We were a mess, and we shared our messy lives, and messy relationships with one another. Through our honesty, sharing, and prayer, God met us and taught us about Him and about ourselves.

As mothers of teenagers, we were at times broken. Our hearts walked on two legs outside our bodies, and these kids were scaring us to death. The illusion that we could ultimately control what they chose was shattered. We were afraid and helpless. So not only was God teaching me about my thoughts, feelings, and shame, He was also teaching me how control, and trying to control others, is based on fear. God himself won't even control us. And, here I was continually trying to figure ways of keeping control of my family. I was often far from peace.

Some call it Cognitive Therapy. Yoga practitioners call it Practicing Mindfulness. I've heard it spoken of as, "Thinking about what you are thinking about." But there is more to it than that. The battle was not just in identifying lies, but replacing them with truth. The Bible calls this renewing your mind.

Like every person, my mind had been programmed. I had a lens, a belief system, through which I viewed, reacted and lived life. The problem was that many of my beliefs were just not true. My future, my value, my hopes, and my choices all filtered through this lens. For forty years I believed certain things about myself: the worthlessness, the rejection, the feelings of death and defectiveness, and of course, shame.

Now I had a resource of truth that said some very different things about me than I believed about myself. Huge amounts of information contradicted the belief that I was in charge of everyone and that if I didn't hold it all together, my family would suffer. Unfortunately, having an 'ah-ha' revelation did not overcome the years of programming of negative thoughts. And, so I began to battle. I began to learn how to renew my mind. I became more internally aware, and discovered listening to my feelings was key.

Trapped and frustrated. That is how I felt. I wanted to be done with it all.

Why? Why? Why could it just not all be resolved, "And she lived happily ever after," is the ending I longed for. Because of this system of belief, I found myself trapped in negative cycles, repeating over and over again the same behavior, choices, and thoughts. I did not have trouble when I was filled with happy emotions and circumstances. My troubles would arise when I experienced negative emotions - sadness, stress, anger, frustration, exhaustion, grief, and fear; we all know it and hate it.

Directional flags, and road maps, are how I view these uncomfortable emotions now. Negative feelings are indicators, red flags if you will. There is nothing to concern oneself with if your feelings are of the loving, kind, and positive type. What I found to be key is focusing on the times I would be assailed with negative emotions.

Negative emotions are trying to tell me something. Feelings follow thoughts. Think about this, because it is really important. Feelings follow thoughts. If you feel sad, angry, frustrated or helpless, did it not first originate in your mind? Did you not first ruminate on something that scared you, or that you want to fix, or something about which you feel shame? Can you feel angry, if you have not first had an angry thought? No, it all originates in the mind.

What to do with negative thoughts? First of all, I think our society uses our defense mechanisms to rush to feel good when we should actually be feeling our feelings. We use denial, avoid our legitimate feelings of depression and anger, or just use our most favorite - distraction, to avoid dealing with pain and discomfort. In order to be whole, I needed to spend time grieving and feeling anger.

Being molested by my 'loving' father was a grievous thing. It - and I, deserved to be cried over. I *should* feel anger and rage. What he did to me was shameful. I had never expressed or processed any of this. Sadness and rage were the appropriate emotions for the situation.

For all of us, when something or someone dies, whether it is a loved one, or the death of a relationship such as divorce, grief and anger are the appropriate emotions. When someone disregards your feelings, screams at you, lies to you, or you are in a lose-lose situation, negative emotions should follow. Basically, when someone stomps on your foot, you should say, "Ouch!"

Being stuck in the negative emotions, or believing a lie, which causes the exact same feelings as though the lie were true, is the trouble. There is where the battle lies.

Analyzing, problem solving, and replacing the lie with truth was the process of the battle. I found myself using some of the processes I taught in math problem solving. A common strategy I taught my students was to work backwards when solving a problem. Applying it now in my thoughts looked something like this:

I feel _____ right now. (Negative emotion).

Why do I feel _____?

What have I been thinking about?

When did this feeling start?

What occurred right before the feeling?

What is the belief or thought behind the feeling?
(Ponder this. Then ask.)

- What am I afraid of?
- Is this thought or belief true?
- Does this thought/belief equal what God says about my future, my new identity and me?

If not, renew my mind.

At this point in the problem solving process, I would either let it go as I allowed myself to feel the way I needed to feel, or I would say to myself the truth, what God says about me.

When I felt overwhelmingly oppressed, I said the truth statement aloud. There were times I shouted the truth out loud. These truths were mostly from the Bible and sometimes just from me.

Some examples of truths I used to battle in my mind:

For sexual shame:

- Go away shame, I am free in my marriage bed.
- God wants me to enjoy my husband; I choose to love him now.
- Old things have passed away and all things are made new. Shame leave me, you have no place here.
- Thoughts of my dad leave me now in the name of Jesus.
- It is for freedom that Christ has set me free.

When I feared something terrible would happen to my family or me:

- If God be for me who can be against me?
- With long life will He satisfy me and show me his Salvation.
- For I know the plans God has for_____, plans not to harm _____, but to give _____ a hope and a future.
- God will never stop doing me good.
- No eye has seen, no ear has heard, the things God has prepared for _____ because he loves _____.

For the nameless feeling of defectiveness and 'unlovableness':
- I am the beautiful one whom God loves.
- I am perfect and God delights in me.
- I am your beloved and you are mine and your banner over me is love.
- You formed me in my mother's womb, and before I was born, you knew me.

For the fear of missing God and that I needed to work to be perfect:

- He who began a good work in me will see it through to completion.
- God is the AUTHOR and FINISHER of my faith.
- It is God at work to WILL and to DO according to His purpose.
- Even if your heart condemns you, God is greater than your heart.
- He will cause me to walk in his ways.

The fail proof renewing your mind prayer of all is:
- Satan, leave my mind. You have no place here, in the name of Jesus. I am His. Go! Now!

And, so the battle continued. Now to be honest, my beliefs

did not change overnight. In fact, it is a mystery to me how the power of God has worked to change my thoughts, my beliefs, and me. But over time, it has sunk in. At first, though I might say I was the beloved of God, it didn't feel like it. Many, many times as I renewed my mind, my thoughts would instantly change, but it did not stick. In my deepest heart, it did not saturate into my core. Stating these affirmations has been an act of faith.

Somehow, slowly, my filter of belief changed. I still renew my mind, but it is not a battle. I truly believe all of the affirmations above, so now my subconscious agrees that all of the above is true.

CHAPTER 27

Just Say No to Codependency

Perfect love casts out all fear, because fear has to do with punishment. The one who fears has not been made perfect in love.

—John 4:18

A DREAM ONCE AGAIN initiated the revelation. As I slept, my dad handed me a library book and told me to read it. It was blue and had white writing and the title *Boundaries* was distinctive. Vividly detailed, I recalled each part of the dream as I awoke. The next day I went to the library and asked if they had heard of a book called *Boundaries* and low and behold, the exact book from my dreams was there. It was actually called *Boundaries, When to Say Yes and When to Say No to Take Control of your Life*, authored by Dr. Henry Cloud and Dr. John Townsend.

When to say yes or no to take control of my life? Why should I read this? Did I lack control? I would say that I was extremely controlled. I planned out everything - for everyone. As I began reading, another dawning ensued. I was overly controlling, and that was part of the problem.

'No' was a dirty word in my vocabulary. My unwillingness to own my desires, resulted in me saying "yes" to things I shouldn't involve myself in or didn't want to do. I was well meaning, but had a twisted definition of love. Love was making others happy and helping others have happiness. If everyone I cared about was happy, then I was happy.

Why was this bad? Where had this belief about love come from? As the victim of sexual abuse, my boundaries were violated in the most basic way. This violation, and having to make sense of it as a child, caused me to form beliefs that I must sacrifice or give, even when I don't want to. My purpose was to gratify others.

We know Jesus is the Savior, but I believed myself to be the savior of my family. I did not want anyone I loved to experience pain or suffering and especially not to be hurt or abused. This desire, to avoid suffering, caused me to intervene in many situations that were not my business. This might sound loving, but it was actually selfish. Because I cared about others and lacked boundaries, their suffering felt like it was happening to me, I didn't want to suffer their choices. I would influence, hint, and manipulate in what should have been the free choice of others, because if they suffered, I would suffer. Not only did I want to help my family avoid pain, but also taking care of strangers was my business.

An example of this was one of the times I gave a brand new acquaintance money to help with her bills. We met and engaged in a dialogue during a children's camp, where, in casual conversation, she shared she was struggling financially. *Perfect I thought, just the divine encounter I've been praying for to help the needy, $1,000.00* *should do it.* It felt so good to save the day..."*Datadadah! Super Chris to the rescue!*

Two months later, she called me this time, asking me for money. A few months later, she called again. It did not feel like a divine encounter this time. It felt like I had gotten enmeshed with someone who did not know how to handle finances. What to do? Was I going to be her savior again? Was my help helping at all? Was I preventing her from experiencing the natural consequences in life that bring forth learning and self-discipline? A year later we watched as she was being arrested for putting a second pair of jeans over her pants at Wal-Mart as she shop lifted.

Encounters like these taught me that just because there is a perceived need it is not my obligation to meet the need. As I continue to deal with my codependency, my definition of love has changed. I believe God wants our highest good.

Loving myself means I make choices for my highest good. Resting, relaxing, letting myself off the hook when needed, but especially in choosing relationships that are good for me, this is how I love myself. In my family system, we were taught that what happens in the family stays in the family. Love is staying with one another no matter what, and keeping quiet to protect the reputation of the family is of prime importance.

I have since learned that this is the litmus test for abuse. It is called the, "Don't Talk Rule." Basically, the abuse: verbal, sexual, emotional or neglect is not the problem, talking about it is the problem.

Think about it. With abused women, the problem or issue of conflict in the home often becomes that the victim called the police, not that they are getting knocked around by their spouse. Kids are called finks if they report bullying, shifting the issue from the bullying behavior as the problem, to the telling an authority figure. Telling about the abuse becomes shameful, not the act itself. I remember mentioning to my dad that I had said something about his visiting my mother's best friend and getting chewed out for talking about the family. "What happens in our home, stays in our home," he had said. The message was, if you love your family, you don't tell its secrets.

Now as I learn to love myself first, I want to be with people who make me better. When I get finished hanging out with family, friends, or church members, do I feel good about myself? Feeling drained and exhausted, like the life was sucked out of me in certain relationships, became a sign that I needed to set limits or end the friendship altogether. Feeling condemned after hanging out with well-meaning Christian friends was another sign. God himself does not condemn, so I needed to evaluate if I was trying to fulfill another's expectations, rather than God's. I make choices now to love myself because I am valuable and what I feel matters.

My codependency and enmeshment with my kids was huge. I was scared my children would not grow up to have a close relationship with God. I was the 'Jr. Holy Spirit' in their lives, telling them about their wrongs. I remember crying out to God and telling him that I can make my kids say the words, "I'm sorry," but that I couldn't make them feel repentant. I remember God telling me that it was not my job. My job was to give appropriate consequences and that he was in charge of the heart. I discovered I was making them hate God and was putting higher standards on them than God himself does…all in the name of God. This is Spiritual Abuse and I was the perpetrator.

The bottom line was that I did not trust God. I did not believe that God was good. I did not believe God would cause good to come from every painful situation in my life, my kid's lives, and everyone else's. People would always say, "You just gotta trust God." *Really*? *How easy is that*? These well-meaning folks must believe that God is good, but I was not there.

When something truly scary would come up, like a seriously ill child or my son joining the military, I would finally just admit to God that I did not trust Him, but that I was going to try. I would have to humble myself and tell Him that ultimately, I did not have a choice, since I wasn't in control. Teenagers will reveal this: I AM NOT IN CONTROL. It was more comforting to me to be honest with God than to try to fake it. I have found that just acknowledging my lack of control helps with the anxiety. The life-long journey of this world is continually learning that God is actually good, and will cause good to happen in every situation.

Weight lifting. That is what this process is like. The trust muscle is weak. As I acknowledged my weakness and letting go to His goodness, He came through. Time and again He came through. At times it was not as I would have directed Him, yet I discovered He is a lot smarter than me. I no longer use the one-pound hand weights, but I can't bench-press my body weight either, as I continue this life-long journey of trust.

The best, very best gift I got from reading this book, *Boundaries*, was the "*I want*" part of it. Sounds so obvious, but it is okay for me to want things, say I want or don't want something, and receive respect just because of my desire. I remember when I started using my 'want' with my children.

"Mom, can you take me to the store?" child asks.

"No," was my reply.

"Why not?" child asks.

"Because I don't want to," was my reply.

Dumbfounded look from child.

Healthy people are going to be like "duh." But for me, I could never say no unless I explained a reason - to everyone. There was a silent, yet vocal 'should' within me. So often I talked myself out of my first instinctual "no," and believing if I said "no," I needed to have a reason. An underlying resentment would build in me because I was overly committed to things I did not want to do. I cannot tell you how many justifications I have felt obligated to give, only to be followed by caving in to other's desires and expectations. As soon as I gave a reason, then I opened myself up to defending the validity of my reason. But, "I don't want to".... no argument. You want what you want.

As I write this, I am very aware that I have not arrived. This area, especially, continues to be a problem for me. One of God's promises is that, "He gives you the desire of your heart." It has been very, very difficult to get in touch with my desires, because my overriding desire is to make everyone happy, have no one upset with me, and be liked. I was such a perfectionist and sought love and admiration from everybody - *everybody*. I care/cared what everyone thought. Owning my aspirations and inclinations, my likes and dislikes, my wants and desires connects me to my authentic self.

Silencing the voice that tells me I am selfish for wanting things, for having preferences; that I must 'do' is so important. Authentic Chris accepts: I am pretty enough, smart enough, kind enough, and spiritual enough right now in this moment. I have come to trust and embrace *me*, flawed, but wonderful as I am. I have stopped trying to change and improve myself, to create the most perfect version of Chris possible. I embrace God's plan for me and my feelings in the moment, realizing God's plan for me will not be something

I will hate. Therefore, if I am asked to do something I don't want to do, I say "no." I trust that I *want* what God wants for me. Not that life is always easy, but His plan will not make me miserable.

The authentic me believes His plan for me will utilize my natural abilities, as well as my struggles, in a way that is enjoyable and makes me happy.

Understanding codependency has done so much to free me from self-pity and the victim mentality. It is so easy to fall into the 'poor little victim' role. My red flags are, " I can't" and "I have to." We all know when we are talking to a victim. They complain and whine about what frustrates them. When possible solutions and scenarios are offered, they always refute any possible choices for change. The key words are, "couldn't, can't and have to."

I can, and, No, I don't have to; those are the truth. I don't have to do *anything* I don't want to do. I choose. I *always* have a choice. I also know that my choices have consequences. People may be disappointed, or angry, or unhappy with my choices, but I still choose. I know that there will be backlash, and a cost with choices that don't please others. This is especially true with those who might be disappointed that I am not rushing to their aid, or am cutting off unhealthy one-way relationships. I am not trapped. Circumstances will happen that I do not like, but I choose how to respond to them. I am no longer a victim. I have choices.

I used to go around rescuing people. My role was to make everyone happy. Because of this understanding of codependency, my definition of love has changed. Love is not making people feel good; it is making choices for their highest good.

This story I would tell my fifth graders is one that illustrates my point.

Little Johnny's mama loved him. Oh how she loved him. She loved to see that sweet little smile on his face and the twinkle of joy in his eye. That mama lived to make her boy happy. Each night she would ask little Johnny if he were ready for bed.

"Johnny, are you sleepy? Time for bed darlin," she would coo.

"Don't wanna go to bed yet," he would mumble.

"Ok, sweetness, as long as you are happy," Mama would reply

She would repeat this hourly until little Johnny would finally fall asleep in front of his video games. After which, she would gently lift her boy and carry him to his bed. She would kiss his cheek, stroke his brow, and tuck him in as she tiptoed from his room.

The next morning she would inquire of Johnny his breakfast desires.

"Darlin boy, would you like some scrambled eggs this morning?" she would sing.

"Don't want eggs, I want ice-cream," he would demand.

"Oh, my most precious boy. Certainly. Whatever you want. I just want to be sure you are happy."

She would reach into the refrigerator being sure to grab the chocolate sauce, whipped cream, and the colored sprinkles he so enjoyed. She would hum a tune about the happiest boy in the world as she prepared his morning meal before school.

When I would finish this story, I would ask my students if Johnny's mama loved him. They would all holler in outrage at me, trying to beat each other to explain why this is not a picture of love. I would play dumb and remind them of how happy Johnny was in the story. He was probably the happiest child on earth to have ice cream for breakfast! I would use this illustration to talk about love and how loving my students would mean that sometimes they might be very unhappy with me, because I wanted them to grow and learn in the coming year.

This example is an extreme, yet when we make choices based on love for another's highest good, the response may not be joy. This means that at times loved ones are going to suffer. They will get the consequences for their choices and have the opportunity to learn from their mistakes. I am still learning that I am not the savior to others; I have a Savior named Jesus. He is enough. I can let go and trust Him.

CHAPTER 28

The Present

For I am convinced that neither death nor life, neither angels nor demons, neither the present nor the future, nor any powers, neither height nor depth, nor anything else in all creation, will be able to separate us from the love of God that is in Christ Jesus our Lord.

—Romans 8:38-39

LOOKING OVER MY SHOULDER at the path I have traveled, I'm in awe. Embarrassed tears used to flow if I even tried to speak of the abuse. Never in my wildest imaginings did I think I could be healed enough to want to speak, to want to write to bring forth light, to want to help others with their pain. I was in too much pain myself.

Authentic, real, transparent, me…that is how I aim to live now. The road to healing is a hard one, but it has been worth the effort. My words of advice to those who share the journey:

"You are in pain every day, anyway, from the consequences of the abuse, the pain just comes out in subterfuge. Why not face the big pain and allow healing? Like a festering splinter, it is so painful every time it is touched; you just want to leave it alone. But, only by enduring the pain of squeezing out the infection and pulling out the wood will it get better. Face the big pain, little by little with Jesus by your side. He is the most gentle of healers and will hold you close as you allow Him to touch those tender, hidden places."

My life is happy and I mostly rest in peace. Relationships can be messy, but they are so much healthier than before.

I am currently enjoying a redemptive phase with my adult children. Thank God He fixes and restores my parenting mistakes. There were times that my kids withdrew from me and hated my interpretation of God. I have apologized and spoken from my heart. My past is known to them and they get where I have been. Like my own mom, "I did the best I could." God did not allow me to be the mom I wanted to be. I couldn't meet all their needs the way I wanted to. If so, they would have been perfectly loved, perfectly safe, and perfectly happy. They would have had no need for God at all!

There is pain, though, as they make their way in life. It hurts to see your children broken. We've heard the expression, "Little kids, little problems. Big kids, big problems." It tears at ones heart that we can't fix the big boo-boos of adulthood for our children.

Learning to let go, I have discovered that in their trials, God has been faithful. Finally, through surrender, I have my heart's desire for my kids. In their brokenness, they have their own God. They have found Him, for Himself, and for themselves. He loves them. He answers them. And, I keep my big mouth out of it and just smile and quietly sing in my heart when they share their journey of faith.

This book is the most courageous thing I have ever done. I have been willing to bare my soul to some very unsavory things.

I am willing to be naked, if my being stripped bare can help someone else.

If even one person reads this and can identify with my journey, and because of my sharing, allow Jesus to begin healing them, it will all be worth it. This will be my redemption, the good coming from something bad.

> *"Satan meant it for evil, but God worked it for good."*
> *—Genesis 50:20*

My desire is to bring dialogue and healing – not just in the area of sexual abuse, but for any inner pain of the heart within the heart - hiding in the shadows blocks healing. There is so much hope for those who suffer silently. I hope, too, that those in the church who have not been molested would read this book and gain insight into the trauma and the impact of trauma. There are so many gifts of the Spirit sitting dormant and underutilized in the Church. By understanding that as soon as a victim shares even a part of their story, shame will immediately attack, would help victims immensely. Being able to speak words of Grace and truth as the shame arises is huge to break the prison of silence. Understanding this, and addressing it, would go far in helping victims receive Jesus as they heal.

I dream of Sunday school classes or small groups where victims gather together, or better yet, a class that is called, *Processing the Past in Faith.* Any kind of past pains could be shared and healing would begin. I imagine the gatherings being no big deal, like a grief group, or 'Divorce Care.' There would be some further along the path of healing bringing forth good from the evil done against them. Receiving all God has for us, as well as working through codependency, would be the focus. Above all, there would be prayer

118

and support. It would be a safe place where the "Don't talk" rule is broken and it would "be okay to not be okay."

My fantasy is that by speaking about the unspeakable, those outside the church might come in. I fantasize and see myself as a hostess to the hurting. I throw great parties and Jesus is reported to being quite the partier Himself. I imagine the introduction, "Hello, lost, abandoned and used, let me introduce you to my friend Jesus, the King of Forever."

More than ever now, my eyes are open to see all the good and beauty around me. I embrace the things I love, like dance. I am a dancin' fool and Jazzercise is my favorite exercise. I will join in any chance I get. I no longer care if I look silly at 55 getting my groove on. When I dance, I feel so sorry for those on the sidelines. I feel the yearning radiating from them. They are half judgmental, that the dancers look ridiculous, and half envious because they are free to move, unencumbered by self-consciousness, having fun, full of joy, and with little regard as to the thoughts of those on the sidelines of life.

The phrase running through my head right now is "showing up for life." We can't know the outcome of each step we take, but we can just Go!... get out there and see what happens. Rather than hiding and avoiding others, show up... hit the road, leave for the journey. Go to the dance.

I currently live a quiet, introspective life. I have an extroverted side, but it lies mostly dormant right now as I am in a season of waiting and reflection...and, that is ok. I am learning to be content in each season. With all that is going on in the world, I look at my peace with amazement. Terror attacks and natural disasters have little affect on my peace. I am not afraid. I am safe now. When I begin to get stirred up or worried, I remind God that I am His kid. It is his job to take care of me, to direct me, and to communicate with me in a way that I understand. After trying to do it all, I treasure my littleness. His power is made perfect in weakness. How easy is that? I can be weak. I am weak – and, I embrace it.

CHAPTER 29

The Dance

Listen…lean in…
Do you hear the melody of your heart?
The yearning?
The King is calling.
Wooing with a song.
A song He sings over you, about you, just for you - your song.
His hand is outstretched…
"Come along, sweetness."
"Come and be held."
"Come and be known."
"Come be mine."
"No longer are you the silent wallflower,
angry, afraid, and alone."
"The Bride price has been paid and I choose You."
"You."
"The real you."
Embrace your song.
Embrace the sway.

The rhythm. The beat.
Dance your dance,
-The one you alone can do.
"The chains are broken, your beauty unveiled."
Eternal lightness,
Joyous,
Radiant,
'You are my dancing bride,
mine forever."

Epilogue

WE ARE FORMED IN our mother's womb for His love, to know love, and to share love. Each one of us is His little one, created in uniqueness with our individual quirks, and distinct beauty. The plan is for us to receive love, so we can share love. Each person has gifts, talents, and people to love and no one else can take our place to accomplish what we alone are meant for.

Each of us is glorious, beautiful, and divine. Think of the radiance of light that streams through the clouds. We can glimpse individual beams of light at times, knowing that we are seeing something extraordinary. We know that the individual rays we see are but one tiny piece of radiance of an infinitely larger and more radiant sun. This is how I think God sees His beloved, His little ones - individually glorious, but sharing and united in the bigger beauty of Him.

When we look at the stories in the Bible, we see tale after tale where forces of evil tried to destroy the beloved, the anointed, or chosen of God.

Baby Moses was placed in a basket to float down a river to save him from death. Joseph's brothers threw him in a pit, hoping he would die. Saul tried to kill David, the anointed King of Israel. And, Jesus himself had to be hidden in Egypt when he was a tiny infant, to avoid being killed. Basically, there is an agenda of evil against us all. The agenda is intended to prevent us from fully receiving God's love for us, to damage us, and to keep us trapped in lies, to keep us from God's true purpose for our lives – plans to prosper us and fulfill us. Above all, to stop us from having the abundant life of joy and adventure God has planned for us.

You may have a story like mine. The beloved baby was born, evil came to destroy the beloved. Now, we embrace our unique authentic self, because we were beloved from the start.

Sexual abuse is one agenda of Satan to wound and destroy God's beloved. I have written this book because I care about my fellow survivors and I believe that God is bringing the fullness of His abundant life to those who might be stuck in the pain of abuse. My goal of this book is to demonstrate through my own story what actually happens to the heart, and how the soul of victims is fragmented, and some might even say murdered, during childhood sexual abuse. I hope I have demonstrated that the attacks of the enemy can create a hidden heart within the heart. By being honest about the damage, my purpose is to bring hope, healing, and restoration.

This book is about receiving. I am convinced that multitudes of Christians love God, serve God, and are His, yet have not fully received all of the Love God has for them. Of course, the Love of God is infinite, and truly immeasurable. Yet scripture says, that God would have us, "Grasp how high, how wide, and how deep the love of God is for us who believe." We are all on a journey, the same journey; that because we are His, we continue to grow in faith, hope, and of course, love.

This supernatural healing by my Father God has me wondering if perhaps there are others out there who live from the heart, yet have untouched deep places that have not yet received their Abba's love. Perhaps others have pains that go so deep they never allow them to come to the light.

I believe you can't give what you don't have. The desire to love runs deep. Each step we take to love ourselves, receive ourselves, to be kind to and gracious with ourselves, enables us to now give those same things to others.

I hope you will not view this book as a Holy self-scouring, where you work and search to make yourselves better. Rather, my hope is that I impart courage and hope, that my story would inspire praying a few simple prayers and allow our tender, gentle, and good Daddy to slowly uncover and heal places that we may have consciously or unconsciously marked 'off-limits.'

This is not a "How to" book. I have no idea how God is going to work in anyone's life. This is just my story. I have no answers; yet do trust the Holy Spirit, our teacher. You simply have to be willing; willing to let the Father fully in to your heart.

Let me share a dangerous suggestion. Though this is a simple prayer, it may bring about unintended consequences. Trust though, that if you decide to pray this, God is safe, tender and trustworthy, and will show up to show you the way to your own healing and understanding.

Dear Father, If I have an inability to receive all the love you have for me, please heal me. I pray you would bless me with your deep love, that I might love myself more, love others more, and above all love you more. Only you know the deep places of my heart. I remind you that I am just your little kid. I embrace my littleness and open my whole heart to you. I give you my heart and my past; make all things new again.